N.A.C.P. Trilogy
The Final Demagogue
A Novel

♥

Alice McCurdy

Alice McCurdy

Cecil Bay Books
Maryland

Also by Alice McCurdy
N.A.C.P. Notations Admix the Collard Pew
N.A.C.P. II National Association of the Collard
Pew
Nearsighted Child
Inlet the Bible Volume I

Cecil Bay Books
A division of FWOG

♥♥♥♥♥

It was a hot and humid summer July Tuesday morning the breeze was as fresh as Downy rinsed linen hanging on a clothesline pined against the force of the wind.

The grass was beginning to wither so she decided she needed to shower it. Then a shower, a cowboy movie, and a novel to read, and a meal were her plans for the day.

This left her vaguely dissatisfied that she once again found herself without love. Love came to her earlier and would return later.

Stride against the fade of sunlight, she turned on the faucet and noticed the water was not coming out of the holes in the sprinkler.

She walked over to the sprinkler to substantiate her suspicion, as suspected the hose had fallen out of place. It had lost its attachment to the sprinkler.

Next summer she would have a sprinkler system buried in the front lawn.

She bent down to reattach the hose to the sprinkler, soon she heard the sound of a car slowing and precisely pulling into her driveway. She glanced at the driveway. It was a black Escalade.

A man, without immediate recognition, stepped out and headed toward her.

She assumed it was a family lost and searching for the roads that lead to the public beaches. She would give him direction and

♥

continue the task of watering her lawn.

Alyson continued idly trying to reattach the hose to the sprinkler when she felt a sharp blow in the back of her head.

Before she could react, she was being dragged by her hair, across her lawn and into the black SUV by the man who exited the car.

The pounding on her head was as fierce as the sun burning off a tree log. She fought with all her might kicking, biting, and punching.

The man dragged her into the car and she noticed another man who sat in the back seat.

She was forced into the back seat of the car and they both began punching her repeatedly.

Her mouth began to bleed like frozen water thawing from the

warmth into a puddle. Blood leaked from her nose unearthed. Her eyes were sweltered with bruises mind swirling.

They forced her to the floor of the car and tied her hands behind her back and her legs together around her ankles with duck tape.

They taped her eyes shut and her mouth closed.

Then her head was forced in the lap of the man who exited the car. She could barely breathe. She was crippled by fear and she just knew death had come to greet her.

Lost into the sudden burst of the truth, at one point she wanted to die. Death had to have more to offer than the pain she was feeling, but she thought of her children and she gained a surge to live.

♥

She struggled to be set free for a brief moment. Then she thought to strategize. The physical struggle ceased and the mental struggles began.

Alyson struggled to maintain consciousness. She counted sheep in her head as if she was suffering from insomnia.

Before the first right turn she counted 9,000 before the second right turn she counted 3,000, before the third right turn she counted 1,800, and before the first left turn she counted 3,000, and before the second left turn she counted 1,200 and when they came to a stop she had counted 6,000.

Alyson was pulled from the car by her hair and dragged on her knees on hard clay soil into a wooden shelter. She knew it was made of wood because the splinters ripped into her knees purposefully, after she was thrown to the floor. Her knees ached and her body was weak.

A short time later she heard the ribbing of her cotton shorts and the tearing of her blouse open.

She felt the thrusting of a man into her body. He said with contempt, "so this is what you want. Now you have it and how does it feel?" He thrust inside her over and over again. The torment lasted for what seemed like hours.

Finally, everything was quiet and she could hear the mastermind say, "Now leave her to the wolves. She don't taste that good. Maybe she'll make an excellent dinner for them."

The Escalade spun away quickly and she lay in the stillness

♥

of the ostracized dreadful horrendous moment.

She crawled around the floor feeling desperately for a piece of glass, a piece of wood anything her fingers could grasp to try and cut the tape and set her free. Her search was hopeless.

She forced her taped arms to the front of her body by lifting her legs to her chest like an acrobat. She felt the popping in her clavicle and scapula, her shoulder area. But that wound could be mended.

She ribbed the tape from her eyes taking her eyebrows with it and pulled the tape from her mouth. She started with staccato screams. "Help me! Somebody please help me!" But then fear overwhelmed her.

Sweat like drops of blood dripped from her forehead. They, the men may come back. Tanned with freight, she spotted a piece of metal, and with her fingers trembling she cut her hands free.

"Stop the car! Stop the car!" The first lady was on her way to speak at a luncheon for battered women at the University of Virginia. Security leaped from the car commanding the first lady to "Stay put!"

She ignored there command and jumped out of the car straggled from the car like a stack of stuffed envelopes bundled on top of a table, falling inevitable, shouting "Oh my God!

She bent over and lying on the side of the road was a woman, a bruised and battered woman.

Looking through the dried blood on her face, Alyson whispered. "Help me." Within minutes she was air lifted to Richmond Memorial Hospital.

The hospital was prepared for her arrival. A veteran doctor of fifteen years had been assigned her case.

He radioed into the medical helicopter. "What is her status? Her vitals?"

"She has lost a lot of blood, dehydrated, temperature 106 degrees, blood pressure 86/55 and dropping. Heart rate 55 and dropping."

"Give her three counts of … of Demerol."

Right before the helicopter landed on the roof of the hospital and before the four attendants forced her onto a gurney she had already slipped into unconsciousness. Doctor Germaine Ruiz said she was in a semi-coma.

Alyson's mother sat in her brick row home in Philadelphia surrounded by her children and a host of relatives. They had come to comfort her.

It had been a week since Alyson was kidnapped. Prayers and offerings were continually being offered up to God.

Alyson's mother reflected often on the worse day of her life. The day she received that dreadful call from the Sheriff Department.

She was sitting in her house on her blue bellowed love seat, working on a puzzle from the Daily

Newspaper, as a past time, when the telephone rung.

She hollered for someone to answer it. She did not want to break her concentration.

She had retired from a nursing home, having worked for thirty-five years at the same hospital.

She was not one to accept change. She did not take risk and tend to give up easy for "peace sake."

Unlike her daughter Alyson, who strongly believed without equivocation that you speak up for yourself, you fight the side of the right. No wonder she was the president of her high school debate team.

Raising Alyson was easy. Alyson was stubborn and never seemed to understand danger but she made the right choices in life without much guidance. Her curiosity was nerving.

As a mother she remained concern about Alyson's spontaneous reactions toward situations in life.

When shots rang out among gang members in the neighborhood, all her other children ran for cover, but not Alyson. She thought it was her civil duty to find out if anyone was hurt and needed her immediate help.

She never considered the danger first. Delay reactions.

Alyson embraced the bigger picture. She held to her belief system, "no man is an island. If I can help somebody as I travel along this way, then my living shall not be in vain."

She was determined her journey through life would not be in vain.

Someone yelled down the stairs. "Miss Lee the phone."

She hesitated to pick up the receiver, but she was compelled.

She took her Dollar Store reading glasses off her nose and she placed her glasses on her folding worktable. She realized she was sweating.

Reluctantly she answered the call while shouting "I got it! Hang up the phone upstairs! Hello."

"Is this Ms. Lee Santrock?" The voice was loud and stern, demanding.

Hesitating she answered, "Yes."

"Do you have a daughter by the name of Alyson Santrock?"

Her heart dropped before it stopped. Her knees buckled. She collapsed back in the chair.

Softly and nervously she answered. "Yes Sir."

"Ma'am I hate to inform you of this but, it is possible that your daughter has been involved in abduction. If you don't mind, we would like for you to come to Maryland and give us a statement."

"Abduction! Why? Who? Are you sure?" The tears had already begun to flow.

"We don't know Miss. Her neighbor telephoned our office and informed us she saw a group of men force your daughter into a black Escalade, and we'll following up on that lead. Right now we have no more information. Our officers are at the crime scene now doing an analysis of the area."

"Crime scene, analysis." She repeated the officer words primordial. "I'm on my way."

She hung up the telephone in a daze. With her nerves prowling and her thinking incoherent, she could barely remember the telephone numbers of her other children. Her hands were sweaty and her head and heart pounded louder than the rap music coming from her next-door neighbor's teenager's room.

The noise normally would annoy her but it lined up with the force of beat in her head and heart. She dialed a number but she could not remember whose number she dialed.

"Hello." It was Sherry. She recognized her voice. She sounded so much like Alyson.

"Hey. This is your mother. I need someone to drive me to Maryland." She began to cry uncontrollably.

Sherry tried to stay calm so she would not upset her mother any more than she already was, but her heart was palpitating.

She knew if her mother had to go to Maryland on a whelm then something was going amidst with Alyson. "What? Momma what is it?"

"Alyson has been kidnapped."

"My God! Jesus!" Sherry hung up the telephone and drove quickly the five blocks to her mother's house.

Within two hours the family was at Alyson's home, which was now the crime scene. They were told they could not enter the house until the Sheriff Department had completed their investigation.

The Sheriff took Ms. Lee to the side and Sherry followed. She had more information than the rests of the family about Alyson. She was her confidant.

"Do you know of anyone who would have wanted to hurt your daughter for any reason?"

"Yes but I cannot pronounce his name."

Sherry interrupted. "Kweisii Mfumey."

The Sheriff's eyebrows curled. "Why would he want to hurt your sister?" He noticed Sherry was the one to talk to.

"Because she was writing a book about him exposing his dark secrets."

"Do you have a copy of the book?"

"No, but it is somewhere in the house." She pointed in the direction of the house.

An officer approached. He had a manila folder in his hand. "Take a look at this Sheriff."

It was Alyson's manuscript about Kweisii Mfumey.

"Good job." The Sheriff pointed at Sherry. "Stick around. We may need more information."

Sherry and the family were allowed to enter the house. Sherry thought of all the people she would need to inform, to let them know, Alyson was kidnapped. *Oh boy her children.*

Later that night, they turned on the television. The eleven o'clock news was on the television station. The reporter Kia Jackson announced "The Harford Country Police Department has issued an All Points Bulletin, "APB," for Mr. Mfumey. He is wanted for questioning in the missing of a Harford County woman abducted from her home approximately one-thirty three P.M.

Allegedly, this woman was writing a book about Mr. Mfumey, which would have interfered with his run for United States senate.

Details are sketchy and we will inform the viewers as soon as more information is made available. In the meantime, if anyone has any information about this kidnapping please contact the Harford County Police Department."

Carle, Alyson other sister, flipped the channel to CNN. "The police are looking for Kweisii Mfumey in questioning about a missing Harford County, Maryland woman. If you have seen this woman" A picture was displayed. "Or have any information concerning her allege abduction please contact the Harford County Police at 1-555-555-5555."

Mr. Mfumey turned himself into the Harford County Police Department a day after the kidnapping. He was surrounded by a host of lawyers.

He gave a statement that he visited Alyson at her home two days before her abduction. Everything was fine. He had spent the night with her. They were intimate and talked promisingly about their future. She cooked him breakfast. The next morning, he ate and left her house around eleven thirty A.M. and went home.

A week later, Miss Lee received a call. The President of the United States' wife found her daughter along side a Virginia road. She had been air lifted to Richmond Memorial Hospital. "As far as we can tell she is okay."

The family rushed to Virginia. At the hospital, they were greeted by Dr. Ruiz.

He gathered them in the chapel, the lobby was too small to hold the large family, admix tears and sobs, he informed them that Alyson was in a semi-comma. It could takes weeks or months before she recovered and then she could experience post trauma shock, and suffer with temporary amnesia,

Two investigators from Harford County Sheriff Department stood apprehensively in the back of the chapel.

"She is lucky to be alive. Her recovery is up to her. It is up to her if she wants to fight to stay alive or give up. The only thing we can do right now is pray."

Dr. Ruiz was a very handsome man. He had cocoa brown skin, deep dark eyebrows, and round dark brown eyes. He was medium height and slim. His mother was Hawaiian and his dad African-American/Cuban.

He was a wealthy man. His grandfather owned a resort in Maui, Hawaii, which was heir, to him and his mother after his grandfather's sudden death of a heart attack. His parents lived in Hawaii but he settled in Virginia after attending the University of Virginia Medical School.

Dr. Ruiz despised high publicity patients. He had received one of the sniper shooting victims and had to answer a host of questions for the media and the police department. This took away from the value of his profession.

But he had been assigned Alyson's case because the victim was repeatedly beaten and raped. Although he was only a General Practitioner, he had training in Neurology and Gynecology.

The hospital could save money with him as opposed to having three different doctors working on the same patient. "Oh the era of HMOs."

Three family members at a time were allowed to visited Alyson for five minutes. The patient needed to rest. A lot of rest.

Alyson's son insisted on staying at the hospital overnight in the room with his mother. Dr. Ruiz agreed only if he promised not to turn on the television. The patient's brain needed to rest as well. He agreed.

Alyson's daughter remained in Columbia. She would be coming in a few days. The rest of the family stayed in hotels.

The days were long and dreading. Dr. Ruiz's examinations yielded little to no progress. Consequently, the family was looking for a miracle and he could not quench their spirit.

Alyson's heart rate was dangerous low and she showed no signs of coming out of the semi-comma. But Dr. Ruiz trusted her son when he said. "When I call my Mom, when I said 'Momma,' she said 'Uh.'"

So doing a press conference he informed the media. "She's making progress. She is somewhat responsive."

Mr. Mfumey was set free. Although Alyson neighbor identified him in a line up as the man who dragged her into the car, his attorneys argued she got confused, being elderly which day she saw him.

She was white and they claimed she believed "all of us look alike."

With Alyson in a semi-comma and no other witnesses, Key was set free to walk the streets of Baltimore preying.

———

Dr. Germaine Ruiz was on his ranch sitting in his lanai facing the mackerel skies, with his back to his Virginia historical mansion, glaring out in the dark abyss of the night.

Neither the stars nor the moon added any light.

Sleep had escaped him. He had printed a picture of Alyson off the Internet and framed it. The picture that was flashed on all the television channels and news stations when she went missing had compelled him to print and frame it.

He vowed to restore her to that beautiful face and person if at all possible.

There was something about her eyes. What did they say or not say? They were a mystery.

She knew the danger of writing this book yet she was willing to take the risk.

She could have wrote the material as a ghostwriter using a pseudonym. Why or why not?

Dr. Ruiz felt compelled to go check on his patient. He drove the sixty miles to the hospital while listening to a talk show on his car radio.

It was a radio station out of Baltimore replaying an earlier interview with Mr. Mfumey. He was surprised he was able to get a reception.

Mr. Mfumey arrogantly declared his innocence from the mountaintop to the valley low. But somehow Dr. Ruiz got the intuition Mr. Mfumey was loving every bit of the attention he was getting, whether it was negative or positive.

The entire ordeal, Alyson being abducted, beaten and raped, Mr. Mfumey, a prominent black icon that Dr. Ruiz had admire for years possibly being the suspect, was absurd.

Dr. Ruiz arrived at the hospital five past three A.M. He walked past the lobby and in there sleeping was Alyson's son with the television on. Dr. Ruiz smiled.

He had one of the nurses cover the young man with a warmed blanket.

Mitose loved his mother and wanted to reach out to her. He was helpless without her.

Dr. Ruiz vowed she must recover. Dr. Ruiz wanted to reach out to Mitose, Alyson's son in more ways than one. But he had to stay professional.

Dr. Ruiz walked in Alyson's dark room. He read her vitals. For the first time he noticed improvement.

He spotted a brush on the table next to Alyson's hospital bed and on impulse before he could control himself he picked the brush up and started brushing her hair.

While he brushed her hair a song rang through her head. He kissed her forehead and said, "You can pull through this. You're strong. Your son needs you."

Dr. Ruiz walked over to the window. The night was still darken. It was a full moon. It's funny how light scattered dark but there was no light in that night.

He turned back and moved toward the patient's bed. It startled him when he looked down at her and she was staring back at him.

"Hey. Welcome back." She was motionless and closed her eyes to return to her world. He summed up the eye opening was involuntary eye movement.

Dr. Ruiz returned to his home around five o'clock in the morning. He could not sleep. He picked up the telephone and dialed his father in Hawaii. He was a doctor too.

"Hey Dad." He knew his dad would answer the telephone in case it was the hospital calling him in. His mother slept well at night.

"If you had a patient in which you found yourself doing things different than the norm what would you do?"

"Every patient is to be treated different. Each one has his or her own unique special needs. That's normal."

"No, Dad I mean going to the hospital three A.M. and losing sleep over this patient, brushing her hair, kissing her forehead."

"Oh my."

"Should I withdraw as her doctor?"

"What do you think? Are you taking about the Alyson lady?"

"Yes."

"Pretty girl."

"What's new?" Dr. Ruiz had his share of pretty women.

"Well, if you don't start making unethical medical decisions based on emotions instead of professional training, you should be fine. Don't sweat it."

"Thanks Dad."

Dr. Ruiz arrived at the hospital that same morning eleven fifteen A.M. Alyson's daughter, grandson, and ex-husband were coming in from Columbia.

Alyson's mother had requested that he be present to assist with explaining to her thirteen year old daughter the medical condition of her mother.

When he arrived he found her ex-husband, an older man, much older than she, tall, trimmed hair, tidily dressed and a precious little girl, very pretty, quiet, seem to desire assurance of safety, her mother's eyes and father's hands, and a talkative grandson, wide eyes and slender, merry, he met no strangers, held expectation of delight, inquisitive, how Dr. Ruiz had imagined Alyson in her conscious state.

"Where is my grandma? I want to see my grandma."

The grandson's mom spoke to him. "In a minute Da-Da."

She had a strong southern accent, face narrowed, attractive, and she inhaled deeply, stiffened. She was trying to control her emotions.

Dr. Ruiz explained to Tazzy, Alyson's daughter, gently, "her mother was in a deep sleep so when you talk to her she won't respond or answer you but she can hear you. So be patient."

In addition he explained that her mother did not look the way she was use to seeing her but her face would return to normal in a few weeks. Without saying, he wished without plastic surgery.

Along side the ex-husband, with his patient's mother and father, two of her sisters, her son, grandson, his mother, and her daughter, Dr. Ruiz escorted them to Alyson's hospital room.

Tazzy took one look at her mother and began screaming and ran out of the room. Her brother chased after her. The others stood around the room crying.

"That's not my grandma." Her grandson was confused.

"Yes it is baby. Grandma has had an accident. She'll be okay." His mother explained.

Dr. Ruiz struggled to hold back tears.

Da-Da walked over to his grandmother's hospital bed and full of love he leaned over and whispered in her ear. "Grandma your baby is here."

Alyson turned her head toward his voice and her eyes opened. Dr. Ruiz was afraid it was another involuntarily eye movement and would give the family false hope, but she stared at her grandson and then she smiled.

The despondent tears turned to tears of jubilee. Everybody shouted and cheered. Mitose returned with Tazzy. Tazzy moved slowly and with caution toward her mother.

Mitose picked her up and the two of them hugged their mother and cried. She struggled to speak. "It'll be all right."

She encouraged her family. Family was called from near and far. Their prayers had been answered. This renewed their faith in God.

Dr. Ruiz cleared the room to examine his patient. She had enough strength to meet with the police investigators for five minutes. They had been waiting for her recovery.

She agreed to meet with them; briefly, she could barely speak so they would communicate non-verbally.

Officer Starks spoke, "I'm going to show you some pictures. I need you to nod or shake your head if these are the men who did this to you."

He showed her a picture of Mr. Mfumey. She nodded.

He showed her a picture of Mr. Saul Carll. She nodded again.

"These are the men." She nodded once more. He was relieved.

Alyson was trying to say something else but she could not get it out. Dr. Ruiz interrupted thinking she had enough. "That's all for today." The investigators left to meet the press.

She motioned for Dr. Ruiz to hand her a pen and pad. She wrote down some words. Dr. Ruiz read the note and exited the room quickly.

A press conference was held in front of the hospital's emergency entrance on a makeshift podium, thirty minutes after Alyson identified her perpetrators. Dr. Ruiz, Officer Starks and his assistance stood on the podium before a bank of microphones pressed against their mouths.

Dr. Ruiz spoke first. He started by thanking everyone for being so patient with the hospital and their staff and for allowing them to do their job. Then he unfolded the note Alyson had handed him, with trembling hands he announced "this note is from Alyson Santrock, please bear with me" and with difficulty he began to read. "Circumstances withstanding, first and foremost I would like to take this time to thank the almighty God for holding back the death angel. Secondly, I would like to thank the hospital staff, Dr. Ruiz, the nurses, nurse's aides, housekeepers, dietitians, and all others for taking such good care of my family and me. Thirdly, I would like to thank my family, friends and the American people for their prayers and gifts. Lastly, but not least, I would like to thank the United States of America's first lady for her kind spirit. May God bless you all so we may continue to fight for the right and conquer the wrong. With all my heart, thank you."

Dr. Ruiz took a step back and Officer Starks took his place at the mikes, "I would like to announce Mr. Kweisii Mfumey and Mr. Saul Carll Swanne are being arrested on Abduction, Assault and Battery with intent to kill and rape charges."

Psychiatrists spent the next several days in sessions with Alyson from both sides of the fence, the prosecutor and defense. They summed up the sessions, as "patient is unable to recall any events prior to being pulled into the car."

Key and Saul's defense team decided they wanted a jury trial. They believed they had a good case. Alyson was suffering from amnesia. She never saw her abductors' faces. They could win this case.

A week after coming out of her comma, Alyson started demanding to go home. Her mother wanted her to come to her house and Dr. Ruiz thought that was a good idea, but she refused.

Dr. Ruiz sat on the edge of her bed, while she packed to go home, after being discharged from the hospital.

He was puzzled. "Why won't you go to your mom's house? The

police don't know if others are involved in this crime."

"Because I refuse to allow them to control my life. If I allow them to control where I live and what I do then I'm living for them and not for me. I have to do what I believe is right no matter how serious the consequences. When the time is right all things will be revealed."

Dr. Ruiz understood why she insisted on writing that dangerous book. She was courageous. He admired her.

"What do we do with all the stuffed animals people have sent you? We have a storage closet full."

"You know I've always wanted to start a program within the Foster Care System named 'Bearly Friend.' I believe each foster care child should have a friend to travel with them through the journey to and hopefully from the Foster Care System.

This way they would have something to confine in. Donate them to the Virginia State Foster Care Program and tell them to make sure all foster care children get a bearly friend."

Dr. Ruiz reigned Alyson's impregnable heart of gold. He thought how could someone hurt such an honest and conscientious human being?

Alyson arrived home within four hours after her conversation with Dr. Ruiz. A song was corded in her temporal. So she wrote the words to the sung on a notepad 9,000 right turn, 3,000 second right, 1,800 turn right again, 3,000 turn left, 1,200 turn second left, 6,000 stop.

She picked up the telephoned and dialed the Sheriff Department. Once Officer Starks picked up the telephone, his voice discontinued the music. Alyson echoed in a monoclinic tone, "I think I know how to get back to the scene of the crime."

With officers escorting her, she took the rough retrograde nullified ride with a scarf tied around her eyes and her emotions stride. The visual affects would blur her concentration. She counted 9,000 then the officer turned right, she counted 3,000 and he turned right, 1,800 he turned right again 3,000 turn left, 1,200 he turned second left again, 6,000 he stopped. The shed was gone. It was burned down.

The jury trial started eight months after Alyson's abduction. The prosecutor presented their case to the jurors.

The DNA showed Key and Alyson had sex but Mr. Mfumey had stated they were consensually intimate two days prior to the abduction.

Alyson's neighbor took the stand but under cross-examination she could not say she was one hundred percent sure it was Mr. Mfumey who forced Alyson into the car. "It all happened so fast."

She said she did not see the other men. The windows were tinted.

It was risky. But the prosecutor had to put Alyson on the stand and let her at least attempt to tell what she recalled. Hopefully, the jury would sympathized with her and make someone pay for this crime.

"Do you swear to tell the truth the whole truth and nothing but the truth." The bailiff wrung out the words as if he was performing an ode.

With her right hand on the Bible Alyson stated confidently. "I affirm."

The prosecutor spoke: "Can you please tell the jury what happened to you on April 1, approximately thirty-three minutes past one P.M.

"I was in my yard trying to water my lawn when a black Escalade drove up…"

It was the defense turn to cross-examine Alyson. "Ms. Alyson we are so sorry for the horrendous thing that has happened to you but in all honesty you don't remember a thing."

"I do!"

"No you don't! Didn't the prosecutor show you a picture of my clients fresh out of a comma, when you barely could speak and told you these are the men who kidnapped you?"

"No sir. They showed me pictures but."

"Didn't you tell both the prosecutor and defense psychiatrists that you cannot remember anything after being pulled into the car?"

"No sir!"

"Oh you didn't! May I approach the witness your Honor?"

"Yes you may." The judge gave permission.

♥

"In exhibit F line 33 read that please for the jury." He points to some words on a piece of paper.

"Client was unable to recall events after being pulled into the car."

The defense attorney raises his voice to make sure everyone in the courtroom heard him. "Client was unable to recall events after being pulled into the car."

"Yes, but it's not a quote. It is a psychiatric assessment. I did not say to the psychiatrists I do not remember I just stopped talking when we got to that point. It was too painful."

"No further questions your Honor."

Alyson made an attempt to continue. "I remember…"

"No further questions your Honor!"

Key sat erect in his chair. His face smugly frozen with discernment and hands icy. The mayhem tarried.

The judge motioned the prosecutor. "Re-direct."

"Yes. Your Honor I believe I will. What do you remember? Tell the jury exactly what you remember."

Alyson continued. "I remember being in my yard and only concerned about having green grass. I remember trying to connect a hose to the sprinkler system. I remember a black SUV driving up into my driveway. I remember looking at the car, the windows were tinted. I waved 'hi' to Mrs. Blue and waited to hear someone asking for directions to Ocean City. I remember hearing footsteps and I turned to smile and greet the person. I remember the pain from the blow to the back of my head and my hair being torn from my scalp while being dragged on the ground. I remember kicking and screaming and pleading with the man to let me go. I remember being thrown into the black Escalade. I remember screaming, 'what are you doing? Why are you doing this?' I remember glaring at Saul and I remember the demonic look he gave me. I remember Key appearing as a ghoul. I remember thinking they're going to kill me. Panic gripped my throat. I remember hearing the driver; a young dark skinned black man say, 'what are you doing? I did not sign up for this.' I remember the man in the driver's passenger seat, he reminded me of Key, his head was round and face wide and pale with confusion, and his eyes no longer sparkled. He was bulky and athletic and he said timid but passionately 'Man you said you only wanted to talk with her.' I remember Key and Saul Carll slapping me in my face and Saul epically proclaiming 'I hate you. You bitch.' I remember the ripping sound of the tape that bonded my arms and legs and closed my mouth and shut my eyes. I can remember my head being pressed into Key's lap. I could not breathe. Initially I was crippled with fear. I struggled to maintain consciousness. I can remember thinking again I am going to die. I remember wanting to live. I remember counted sheep, the left and the right. The counting gave me solace. I remember being dragged on the cold clay the ground was hard and unfriendly. It scraped my knees. I remember being thrown across the wooden floor and the splinters ripped my skin. I remember the former president and CEO N.A.C.P. mocking me. 'So this is what you want. I'll give you what you want. Are you that angry that I don't want your ass? Write about this.' I remember the pain as he forced himself inside me. I remember the mastermind, Key, opaquely saying 'leave her to the wolves. Maybe they'll find her tasteful.' I remember the black SUV swerving away quickly. I remember the popping and splitting of my clavicle and scapula as I forced my taped arms from the back of my body to the front of my body like a acrobat. I remember ripping the tape off my mouth and ripping the tape from my eyes taking my eyebrows with it. I remember I stood in an empty abandoned shed, with its widow panes chipped, windows broken, foundation unstable and roof collapsing. Blood gushed from my head and blood ran down my legs. The night was vastly approaching."

Tears flowed down the jurors' faces like the river flowed into an ocean. "The wolves' eyes glittered in the distant. I spotted a closet with a door remaining intact. I crawled into the closet for safety. The dark took charge.

I remember throughout the night the incursion of the wolves. They gnawed and hovered at the door for my flesh and blood and I prayed to God to rescue me like he did Daniel out of the lions' den. By morning the wolves were gone. I remember walking in the wheat and cornfields nipping on corn and wheat for days. My stomach churned. I remember climbing in an old pick up truck and praying the owner showed up. My worse fear had been confirmed. My luck ran out. So I had to keep moving."

One juror sobbed audibly. "I remember stumbling walking the long endless road then I could not go any further. I remember the conveying brown eyes of a woman the only words I could muster up was 'help me.' I remember my son calling out to his mother with desertion and trembling in his voice. I remember I tried to respond. I remember a doctor brushing my hair and kissing my forehead and offering me confidence, fulfillment, and reassurance. I remember my mother and father's cries. I remember my daughter's scream. I remember my grandson's words of love full of hope. I remember his words. 'Grandma your baby is here.' I remember, the piercing reality, I would never forget."

Alyson was no longer caught up in a reverie of what should have been. Her nightmare was a reality.

♥♥♥♥♥

The jurors took six hours to

deliberate. The judge asked the defendants to rise; Kweisii Mfumey and Saul Carll Swanne stood smiling with relief.

The arrogant on their faces reflected like the glow of fresh heat. Alyson's nerves stung like a bee sting, Queen Bee.

The judge was handed a piece of paper. Alyson thought about the Michael Jackson trial, if Kweisii and Carll were able to get to one juror with persuasion then they could determine their own fate.

It only took one powerful, persuasive juror and four "I don't care jurors," and three passive jurors and two "let's hurry this thing up" jurors and two angry jurors, "I asked the judge to be set free, I didn't want to set on this trial anyway," and Kweisii and Carll were home free.

The judge read the paper expressionless, and then handed it to the bailiff who handed it to the forewoman, an elderly white lady with white hair, medium size and short.

Alyson had confidence in her when she was placed as a juror, during her life and experiences she had become familiar with men on the down low, but maybe not.

Alyson recalled a book signing in Baltimore. All was going well and she had buddy up with the authors to her right and left.

It was there that she found out that the underground black community already knew Key was on the down low and they were angry with her for exposing him.

They believed she had laid out the black community dirty laundry before the white community. This surprised her.

Alyson sat at the oblong table at the Washington Monument, with her table decorated with figurines. She collected owls. "It's great to be a Temple Owl."

Maybe this was her problem. Had she went to a historical black college maybe she would have been more sensitive to the black community.

It wasn't her fought she was bussed to white schools during the early seventies.

It wasn't her fought her daddy worked for Temple University and they offered tuition reimbursement for undergraduate school. No excuse for choosing Temple University as her graduate school.

She fell in love with Temple University while in undergrad school.

Things could have been worse. She could have followed through with her acceptance into Duke University. If so what would her perspective on the black community had been? Maybe not, her high school sweetheart, a basketball star from Philadelphia chose Duke University for his college. He was the one who prompted her to look at Duke as a possibility for college.

He graduated from Duke University and played professional basketball for a couple years and was very active in the black community.

At the Baltimore Book Fair an older black woman, standing approximately five feet seven weighing in at one hundred and eighty pounds.

She aggressively approached Alyson. Maybe she wasn't as aggressive as supposed. Black women are often perceived as aggressive because they speak with their hands and a lot of non-verbal motions.

Alyson had her share of being falsely accused on jobs, in stores, and other places, as being aggressive when her only attempt was to express herself.

The woman called Alyson a fool for being fooled by Kweisii for so long. She claimed she would not have ever fallen for his tricks.

She knew of another female he had done the same exact thing too. But she had better sense than to write a book about it.

She informed Alyson she should be embarrassed about being deceived by Kweisii and not want other people to know she was a fool. She was abrasive.

But Alyson was unnerved. Her verbal attacks were nothing compared to the "NACP" National Association of the Collard Pew's security physical abuse, coerce by Kweisii and lead by Saul, that infamous day in Miami, Florida.

Alyson defended herself by saying that she believed God let her experience the deceitfulness of Kweisii for a reason and she was willing to share her pain if it would prevent other women from falling into the same trap.

Alyson further said, with calmness, "I'm glad to know that you lived to be in your fifties or sixties and have never been deceived by a man in any way.

Maybe you should write a book so young women like me can learn how to live to be sixty and not get hurt by a man.

Because obviously since you cannot identify with me you have not been hurt by a man before in any form or fashion." The woman was taken aback.

The nerve of her to sympathize with the perpetrator. Doesn't she know women have to stick together against men like Key? We all are potential victims.

She definitely was one of Key's flunkeys. She knew no better. Alyson heart ached for her.

She was caught up in his deceptive web. Maybe one day she'll see the light.

Her eyes opened slightly to the truth. "You know what…to think about it when he speaks he always talks about his momma or grandmother, and I'm wondering what about a wife. He has no concerns for a wife. I'm not saying everybody should get married but."

She paused then continues. "To think about it what man would not be concerned about dating and women even if he does not plan on marrying." She walked away puzzled by the hard hit of reality.

The forewoman stood while the other jurors sat. She opened the paper and glared at it as if it was foreign to her.

"On the count of kidnapping, Guilty. On the count of assault and battery with intent to kill. Guilty. Rape charge, not guilty."

Alyson was startled by the rape not guilty verdict but pleased with the other guilty verdicts. She breathed a sigh of relief. She would be free of Mr. Mfumey for years to come.

No more brawling noises outside her home. No more trembling fingers dialing the Police Department three A.M. in the morning. No more Sheriff cars sitting outside her home, on twenty-four hour watch. She would be free to live a "normal" life. Finally!

Saul and Key stood stunned without regard. The judge's voice broke Alyson's concentration." Sentencing tomorrow at nine A.M."

Alyson bent over to inquire with the prosecutor. "What are we looking at?" How much time will they get?"

"Wow! They're looking at least twenty-five years, serving at least ten, before eligibility of parole."

"Good."

Alyson now believed if Kweisii had convinced any of his other cronies to complete any hideous acts against her the jury's decision would be a deterrence. Justice had prevailed.

Alyson snuck away from the courthouse quietly, through the back double wooden doors with the gold handles, and into the parking lot guarded by barbed wires and police officers, into a car driven by her older brother and to a disclosed location in Rehoboth Beach.

Alyson had a friend who owned a cottage there. She was staying there until the trial ended and thus the hustle and bustle from the media would ultimately subside.

Maybe Paris Hilton would go back to jail or maybe another call girl like Anna Smith who had the right men on her call list would overdose or maybe Brittney Spears drug addiction would cause more problems than the lost of custody of her children, then the relief would come.

The prosecutors would make contact with her later to inform her what to expect the next day.

Alyson sat outside the cottage. A small three-bedroom cottage surrounded by Azaleas and Deerwood trees overlooking the Atlantic Ocean. It was surrounded by five acres of deer homeland.

It was beautiful to see the deer running so free. Even in death they lacked understanding.

The telephone rung and Prosecutor Melissa Griffin, tall and slim, Caucasian woman, dark hair perky lips and deep dimples, informed Alyson the judge had a lot of leeway in his decision but he would definitely give them at least ten years in prison.

Ten years, by then Alyson would be in her fifties and a lot of changes would have taken place and Mr. Mfumey may become rehabilitated. She could settle for ten years.

The Baltimore courthouse was an old colonial building built in the 1810, home to asbestos, which could be dangerous if disturbed. Its history rich in the injustice of slavery.

The courthouse smelled of mold and wet aluminum, air wick, and old wood.

Since Alyson was kidnapped and attacked by Key she got nauseated at the smell of wood.

The smell reminded her of the wood that split through her knees and the cold shed she laid in seemingly hopeless, the night that never seemed to end.

The air wick reminded of the morning dew that gave her hope when the sun burst into day.

So entering the courtroom the next day for the sentencing of Kweisii and Saul Carll her feelings were ambivalent. She feared the inevitable and hoped for the indefinite.

Everyone sat in the courtroom pensively. *"The judge had too much leeway."* The judge a Caucasian man in his mid-sixties, completed ball, short five foot zero inches tall.

When he entered the court room he stood behind the Judge's bench many days those in attendance in the court room, media, nosey people, or just people unemployment and looking for a way to spend their day, sat before the judge assuming he had already sat down. Alyson found this comical.

The dynamics of the courtroom were ironic. The O.J. Simpson's trial was the first to intrigue Alyson to the antics and dynamics of courtroom activity.

Here O.J. sat on trial for murdering two individuals, and the families of the murder victims sat to his right and yet when Judge Otta said something funny or when the lawyers made a boo-boo, especially the prosecuting team, the victim's families and O.J. was able to laugh.

Alyson could not understand this until she sat in the courtroom a victim and when some of the audience sat thinking the judge had already sat down, she found this funny.

She guessed for all victims at one point the laughter returned, at least one would hope.

Alyson laughter had return but the scars remained visible.

Emotions of fear and doubt crept upon suddenly at awkward moments. For instance entering the courthouse awaiting to embrace the verdicts. The laughter was nowhere to be found. The judge's decision would say a lot.

Judge Tyler Kent ordered Saul Carll Swanne and Kweisii Mfumey to stand. They complied.

Alyson could not help but notice the smirked on Key's face when he quickly glanced her way.

She wondered what was going on. Her instincts ventured. Judge Kent continued. "I hereby sentenced Kweisii Mfumey to ten years, sentences suspended."

The courtroom gasped in disbelief. Alyson was speechless. Her attorneys buried their heads in their hands.

The judge continued, banging his grabble on the desk "Order in the court! Order in the court!"

It took a few minutes then all went silent. "I hereby sentenced Saul Carll Swanne to ten years, sentences suspended." The judge existed the courtroom leaving all to ponder.

Alyson glanced over at the table where Kweisii, Saul and their attorneys stood. They were hi-fiving each other. Laughing. Alyson attorney walked over to the defense team and congratulated them.

Alyson snuck away quietly. Defeated. Alyson thought lady justice was blind. She hoped she could see the corruption in Baltimore because she was an active part in it.

Baltimore was not a good city with a positive reputation. The corruption in Baltimore ranked like the Inner Harbor.

Alyson had informed her attorney that something was fishy for Key's attorney's to ask for a change of venue from Harford County to Baltimore County.

They claim they could not get a fair trail in Harford County because of the percentage of white people and because Alyson presided in that county. Hog wash.

They did not have a judge in their pocketbooks in Harford or they did not have a judge who himself was gay and probably one of Key's lover at one point.

How many men had Key had sex with down through the years? How great was the number of men on the down low? *I bet Key has lovers in so many places. Why are the newspapers so sympathetic to him? They literally wrote all kinds of justifiable reason he should not be convicted. Key probably had lovers on the Newspapers, Editors, on News Station, producers, Banks Presidents, other CEO, everywhere. How could she ever expect to win over a man who knows so much about the secrets lives of so many other men just like him?* These thoughts had hunted Alyson in her nightmares.

Alyson went home. She sat out on her lanai, in her wicker chair, biting on her fingernails. She would not hide anymore. She would not isolate herself from the world.

♥

She felt slightly safe. Maybe Key would leave her alone now. He had won. Surely he would know if anything happened to her he would be the number one target.

Was he cocky enough to believe he was untouchable now? Oh well. Alyson decided "what ever will be will be the future was not hers to see." If Key cut her life short so what. Life was to be lived not feared.

There would be one more trial to be held in Richmond, Virginia, against Kweisii Mfumey with charges of assault and rape. Virginia could not bring kidnapping charges because the kidnapping happened in Maryland.

Was lady justice blind in Virginia? Would she peep through the blinds folds and come out to play and play fair and hard? Only time would tell.

How happy Alyson was that she had not followed Kweisii's advice and found a vacation home in Baltimore. Charm City was a nice place to visit but as told by the movie *The Wire* and the local six o'clock and eleven o'clock news once residency was taken up, the charm was gone, dismantled.

Has anything good come out Baltimore? Sure there has. There are the success stories of individuals who rose above negative circumstances and succeeded in honesty and integrity.

But often enough these individuals sit quietly home minding their own business while the ambitious self-centered individuals seek to rule and control. An attribute of the evildoer.

Living in Maryland, in a rural county miles from Baltimore,

Alyson's city interactions were limited.

She seemed to have escaped the social dynamics of drugs, crime, and educational systems problem; those things alone had deterred her from Baltimore.

Prior to her move to Maryland from the south she started reading the Baltimore Sun via Internet.

After reading there was twenty-five murders within twenty-five consecutive days she decided not to test her fate living in a city ever again, if at all possible.

She had no idea at the time that she was not safe from Key living anywhere. He had too many cronies.

The juxtaposition was only by living in Maryland would or could she learn about the corruption that lurked within the City of Baltimore and surrounding areas, the Governor's extra marital affair with subordinates, which happened to be a close friend of Kweisii.

In addition, the Mayor's extra marital affairs, and the Comptroller flirting with young interns. Allegations on the police force of police officers raping females. Also, the Attorney General's office being bias with who to bring charges against.

The Public Service Commission with the audacity to not being concerned about the public but the interest of corporate America. And yes even the Unemployment Office in the name of protecting the funds, denying hard working people, who had worked for years prior to layoffs, claims even after winning in the appeal process, refusing to pay the unemployment benefits.

Alyson had expected the general corruptions within Equal Employment Opportunity Commission (EEOC). These offices were just a hoax to make Americans believe that America care about discrimination and race relations.

Alyson had conducted a telephone poll and discovered that more white women and gay Americans benefit from this agency than any of the African-Americans who applied. A random sample revealed that sixty percent of gays who filed receive settlements, seven-five percent of white females receive favorable settlements with compensation, but less than one percent of the blacks who applied received compensation.

Americans was on this trend fighting for privatization of agencies. If America really wants to privatize something privatize the EEOC. Compensate attorneys who take these cases. Have attorneys bid for these cases, as they come into the EEOC office, and let's see how discrimination in employment would dwindle down.

Americans really doesn't want to know. Just like the NACP did not want to know that their president was on the down low and deceptive. Let us continue believing in the melting pot.

Alyson summed up the trial in Baltimore by saying "Kweisii had slept with the right men down through the years." Corruption prevailed in Baltimore.

Kweisii believed he was the winner maybe he was. Only time would tell.

Alyson struggled to return to normal. She would seek gainful employment, which should help with her self-esteem.

Maybe she would find work at a company in which no one knew Kweisii. This was limited.

She had strikes against her. Strike one, she lived in a predominant white area in which the only way a black person could find a job if they knew someone to put in a word for them. Alyson knew no one. Then strike two was Kweisii knew people in every state, all fifty, and in the District of Columbia, because of his former position as the president and chief executive officer of the N.A.C.P.

He was abusing his power to

prevent employment for Alyson. She knew it but could not prove it or conquer it.

Maybe she could avoid strike three by branching out into an employment, away from nepotism and out of reach of Kweisii's arms' stretch. Maybe his arms are too short to box with God. Just maybe. Was there such a place other than the land of odds?

Alyson needed to find employment and love. She was young.

Life had a lot to offer. Somewhere out there was a non-gay man who was not under the influence of Kweisii Mfumey.

She had believed "Chip", Artist Yance, with the sparkling eyes standing only a foot shorter than Kweisii, built like an athlete, bow legged, with a smile that lit up his face, to be that man. But his loyalty to his first cousin, Kweisii, proved to be more influential than his liking toward her.

Kweisii's mother and Chip's mother were sisters. Chip was born only one month prior to Kweisii, in August. Kweisii was born in September, the exact same year and same day of the month.

They had grew up as brothers. Alyson did not have the power to break those ties.

Chip was sad to discover that his cousin was a brother on the down low but he could not erase the bind that had kept them throughout their childhood. "Blood was thicker than water."

Alyson was just water running off a cold hard rock in Chip's heart.

For a brief moment Alyson was caught up in the thrill of Chip, but after he unsuccessfully tried to get her to abandoned the publishing of *N.A.C.P. II National Association of the Collard Pew,* he also abandoned the romance. He was good. He did come highly recommended; however, he did turn out to be non-gay.

Alyson was always skeptical about Chip, even before she discovered he was Kweisii's cousin. She never knew if his stories were fiction or non-fiction.

Was he really married for thirty years prior to his divorce? Did he really have five sons and two daughters? Was he really a contractor? What was really the deal?

Because she had no answers to these questions she guarded her heart. His departure was not as devastating as Kweisii. She was just happy he was not gay. Good for him.

It would forever puzzle Alyson why she never told the police that the other guy in the car who sat in the front passenger's seat who eyes no longer sparkled was Chip. Chip would be forgiven. Good for him.

♥♥♥♥♥

Alyson decided to pick back up on her church attendance. She had slacked up prior to and after the accident.

Having a brush with death brought her closer to the understanding and belief in life after death.

She started attending church on a regular basis. She needed to renew her faith in God.

Alyson attended a church with approximately five hundred members on any given Sunday, not too big but not too small.

It was a tin foil warehouse turned into a chapel off a frontage road in the state of Pennsylvania.

It was a hike to drive every Sunday but it had a few black families who attended the service. Unlike the churches in the vicinity of her home her family would be the only black family.

Although Alyson made every attempt to blend with the crowd, this was always an unsuccessfully task of hers.

Maybe because of the red hair or the infusive hazel eyes or broad shy smile but eyes focus on her making her efforts to fade into the shadow impossible.

Alyson decided late entrances and early exists was the only way to avoid being forced to enmesh. For several months, almost a year to date she was successful. Until….

One bright sunny Sunday May day, everything seemed to happen in May, she was approached by a man, a black man. She only knew him by the gold communion plate he handed to her once a month when she decided to break bread with the saints, a requirement as a Christian. He was an attractive man.

Attractive men no longer intrigued Alyson. All her life attractive men had sort her out and been her downfall. Starting with her high school sweetheart, Philly's number one basketball player standing six feet seven, slim and golden skin, the pain of witnessing her two friends bring him children in the world.

Alyson's college sweetheart, one of them, the heartache when she discovered the other women was not lying; he had been dating them too. From there to professional basketball players.

Marcus Checks could you had have any less of women. The telephone calls through the night, the stalking at the movies, out to dinner bust, and the crushing of South streets walks.

At least he was honest "you're the marrying type and I'm not ready for marriage. When I'm ready I'll find you."

He must have never got ready for marriage because he never did find Alyson and he never did get married. Still single to this day. "What's up with that?"

To not marry was selfish any way you slice up the word selfish it fits.

Then Kweisii, an excellent lover, he said all the right things made all the right moves but gay.

Alyson had decided "No thanks! Don't give me fine anymore."

But for this man fine was not fine, maybe nerdy fine. It was difficult for Alyson to grasp and describe.

He was chocolate brown, wore thick glasses but underneath he had nice eyes. His eyes reminded Alyson of the Idris Elba's eyes, the actor from *The Wire, Sometimes in April* and *The Gospel.* Forget Boris Cojo.

Alyson was swept away by Idris Elba. Hc had full lips like Idris and thick eyebrows like Idris. He just needed to smile and if he had Idris' smile Alyson would consider him, if this was the reason he was approaching her.

He wasn't tall. Kweisii's height. But that was okay because he was bow legged and built like he met the gym every morning at 6:00 a.m. with his Multi-Vitamin drink.

"Hi! God bless you." He spoke first.

"God bless you too." Alyson responded

"My name is Wayne Rivers. What's yours?

"Alyson Santrock"

"What?" He tried to pronounce her last name without luck.

"Santrock."

"Oh." He gave up. "I've been noticing you attending our services. We're glad to have you here." He sounded Caucasian but he was Black.

Alyson wondered if he was one of the lost culture black boys. Alyson had ascribed this clique to black people, who subconscious belief "white" was better; therefore, adapting and adopting beliefs and mannerisms of some white America.

The belief that any similarities to the culture of Africa are bambooist and ignorant so I must adjust to my white counterparts in tone and physical behavior. Sad

"I've really enjoyed the services. I'm growing." If only he knew how far she had to grow emotional. The strong wind had beat against her brow.

"That's good to hear. You have a nice week."

He bent over and kissed Alyson on the cheek.

That's it! That's all I get, no what's your number. "Excuse me Miss can I take you out tonight."

A Caucasian man walked up and whispered something to him and they walked away. Alyson had flashes of Kweisii and Carll. Her heart skipped several beats. Her mind took over. *Don't go making this guy gay. Just because Kweisii turned out gay that does not mean he is too. Remember the lady you saw him sitting next too, I bet that's his wife.*

Alyson became full of freight. She had became so weak and lonely that the first man who approached her she was ready to date.

She had forgotten all about the lady who accustomed at his seat every Sunday. Shame on her. But something supernatural had began to occur.

Every Sunday since that May day this middle age deacon, whose name Alyson now knew as Wayne Rivers, watched Alyson from his seat with the lady sitting next to him.

If he was married, Alyson assumed, he must have a weakness. But not being into married men she started to ignore his glares and stares.

For many consecutive Sundays Alyson avoided the deacon. Then loneliness crept in like a snake in the grass and Alyson decided to give the deacon a chance. *No way that lady could be his wife. If he asked for her number she would give it to him. Maybe a dinner and a movie.*

She waiting to here him say, "Excuse me Miss. What's your name? Can I take you out tonight? Because you'll never know where you could find love."

Alyson knew she had to be careful and consciously take it slow. Churchmen, because of the no sex before marriage—fornication—most were not looking for just a date or friendship as she was looking for without haste.

Her experience had been they dated to marry. She had shied away from churchmen in her past.

Growing up in the Pentecostal Faith it was common for individuals to speak in unknown tongue and then interpret the unknown language.

Alyson had her share of ministers, prophets, whatever, which spoke marriage upon her. "You're my wife in the name of Jesus." She had exercise her strength of rebuking those self serving prophesies.

A particular man came to mind. He was short and dark with big lips and unattractive eyes.

He was a young minister at a church Alyson's family's church visited on a regular bases. His name escaped Alyson but the memory lingered on.

He would come to Alyson's annual youth services and proudly sit on the pulpit with the other ministers.

He obviously thought this gave him some prestige.

He was often called to sing solos. He had a beautiful voice. He would sing watching Alyson in lust.

Not into short men and definitely not into ministers Alyson would attempt to avoid his overt flirtations.

Many within Alyson's church, Open to God Pentecostal Church, caution Alyson, including her sister Coral that she was giving up a good man looking on the outside and not the inside.

The outside was very important to Alyson at the time so she ignored their wise folk tale.

Eventually he asked Alyson out to dinner and a movie and annoyingly Alyson refuted his advantages and said "Never!" And then she walked away from him leaving him withered, so she thought.

There was something unusual about his character. It was not only his looks, Alyson found herself despising him, he was repulsive, but what reason she could not understand.

A couple months after Alyson's encounter with him, he was arrested at the high school he worked at. He was working there as a teacher. He had been molesting boys in the closet of the gym room. He hung himself in his prison cell.

What a sad occurrence of events. Alyson was not surprise but felt eerie. At that moment in her life she was wise enough to see the handwriting on the wall. After years of bad relationships and broken dreams her vision became blurred.

Alyson felt with this deacon she would be safe. She had a lot of faith in this organization. They would not promote a gay man in a leadership position. They were spiritually lead men who sort God for guidance.

Alyson believed they were not acting in their own pace.

Although, this deacon had been single for years and his relationship with his mother was peculiar, a momma's boy no doubt, Yes. The lady sitting under his armpits every Sunday morning service was his mother. Not wife.

Alyson had thought for months that his mother was his wife. He caressed her inappropriately and openly. Since these non-verbal acts were committed openly Alyson assumed he was trying to be a "good son" and just did not know how.

Alyson deep down inside was uneasy about his relationship with his mother but she suppressed once again her instincts, which were venturing. He would rub his mother's back and occasionally pull on her bra strap and hug her around the waist just above her buttocks when they stood for worship service.

Alyson suppressed the thought that *maybe he is on the down low and his interaction with his mother are to keep women a bay.*

Alyson studied the pastor of the church reactions toward Wayne and his mother and he did not seem to observe their behavior toward each other as inappropriate, so she brushed off her gut feelings. She was paranoid again.

Would she ever look at a man and see "straight?" Only time would tell.

Alyson held tight to her faith in the leadership of the church.

Alyson was only aware of one suspected brother on the down low, in her youth church, but he had married a girl who all suspected was a lesbian.

So Alyson was not oblivious that gay individuals, for reasons unknown to her, hid in the church. She guessed it was apart of their searching.

When wrong we need someone to condone the behavior, especially if denial was not understood.

Extended from her youth church Alyson had visited churches were gayism, was running rapid from pulpits to the ushers to the janitors.

However, at these churches everyone, unspeakably, knew the truth about each other and were all playing the same game at life. The ministers were in it for the money. The ushers was in it for prestige. The deacon was in it because the pastor was his lover.

If this man was gay he would locate one of the acceptable churches and join not a church with saints, sincerely, no pretentious or hidden agendas other than the honest desire to serve the Lord.

Alyson believe the hurricane had past and another one would not come in the near future. She would believe it safe to desire this man. After months of ignoring him, the avoidance came to a halt.

Alyson purposely made eye contact, giving him the "go signal." If he was normal he would know the difference between "go," "stop," and "yield."

She smiled back when he smiled at her. If a seat happened to be empty on his side she no longer asked for a seat to be made available in the opposite direction.

She took the seat next to him hoping the opportunity would present itself for them to connect.

The first time she sat two rows in front of him she caught his eyes. He smiled. She smiled. His mother glared.

Immediately after service, Alyson agreed she would speak to him. He turned to face another man and seemed to be avoiding her. That hurt slightly.

Alyson was sooooo familiar with the game. But Maria, her best friend and confidant said on the telephone that night that she maybe a little paranoid considering what had happened to her with Kweisii. She would give Wayne the benefit of the doubt. She had her doubts.

Maria and Alyson had been friends for fifteen years. Maria was single, tall and brown, a wise spiritual woman.

Alyson envied her dedication to the service of God. She seemed more in tuned to God than Alyson; therefore, Alyson trusted her spiritual advice.

Alyson was all over the place in her views and thoughts on men since her deceptive relationship with Kweisii "Key" and her physical abuse by Kweisii's lover Saul.

She really felt she did not deserve to be snatched up and thrown all over the floor in her white name brand gown. Kweisii could have been honest and said "I've convinced the board members of the N.A.C.P. that I'm not gay. My contract has been renewed so get the hell away from me." Thus admitting he was using Alyson for that specific purpose.

Maria was madly in love with Tommie Clurk and was faithfully waiting on God to bring him to her. She had met him several times but nothing materialized.

Tommie had admitted to being gay in the past but claimed deliverance from God. But Alyson wondered. She didn't have any faith in gay men being delivered.

Maria said she believed God was powerful enough to set these men free. "Okay," was Alyson response. "An answer of doubt," Maria retorted. Alyson agreed.

Maria felt it was safe to date and marry a man who was delivered from homosexuality.

Alyson believed this was too risky and that these men's gay spirits were too strong to be conquered. She preferred a man without that background.

If the Lord answered her prayer and gave her Tommie, she teased Maria about never trusted him with male friends.

Alyson also told her to time him when he went to the store, or worked out at the gym, or when he visited the men's laboratory, or if they stopped at a rest stop off the highway, please make sure he doesn't go in the bushes in the back. It only takes a few minutes.

Maria was offended. Alyson laughed and admitted she had an issue with trust. Rightfully so.

Accepting Maria's advice Alyson decided to abate the non-trusting spirit, it was crippling.

She decided to give the deacon another try.

One evening service Alyson arrived first. He and his mother came and sat down in front of her. Immediately after service he turned to Alyson and teased about the pastor's sermon.

The pastor had preached about sleeping too much and being late for church. Alyson had responded by saying "Ouch." He heard her. Wayne teased Alyson about being late for church.

Alyson thought *okay this is the moment. All is well.* But, his non-verbal communication ranked. He stood too far away from Alyson. He talked to Alyson but the distance was distracting.

Alyson glanced quickly at the Pastor, Pastor Derek McCoy. The pastor was an Irish man blond with blue eyes. He was blushing at the couple, thinking *they finally got together.*

Alyson instincts told her that Wayne was talking to her because the pressure was on. Alyson was all familiar with the pressure.

Alyson an attractive lady, with hazel eyes, short and petite, intelligent, spiritual, and a fundamentalist was what most men wanted in a woman. If a man did not accept her then it would be obvious to other men something was wrong with him. So Alyson discovered this forced down low brothers to play the game with her.

Alyson went home withered. She gave Maria a call and again Maria said it probably was all in Alyson's mind. Alyson gave her former therapist a call, Crystal Moore, short and overweight, short hair cut but caring and knowing mind, heart, and eyes. She too said Alyson maybe a little paranoid, that it was too few interactions to make any assumptions. Alyson retreated.

Crystal knew Alyson had experienced too many unfortunate things within the past ten years. Kweisii had played with her life a little longer than most down low brother would have; but he had more at stake than most down low brothers.

She had encouraged Alyson to pursue a relationship with Chip, one of

Kweisii investigators who was hired to hinder or stop Alyson from writing her non-fiction book *N.A.C.P. II National Association of the Collard Pew,* assuming he had genuinely started caring for Alyson.

She had to stay up on the telephone with Alyson all night when she found out Chip and Kweisii were first cousins, born the same year, exactly one month apart.

Chip never had any intentions of pursuing a relationship with Alyson.

Crystal prayed to God that this guy Wayne was sincere. She wanted Alyson to learn to love again and to be happy in life.

Maria and Crystal advised Alyson to go a step further. She agreed. "He may be a momma's boy and shy."

That following Sunday, after morning service, Alyson approached Wayne.

She felt this was okay since he had approached her the previous Sunday.

Upon walking toward him Wayne spotted Alyson and ceased his conversation and walked toward her. He grabbed her hand and pulled her toward him and attempted to kiss her on the lips. She turned just in time and he got her side lip and cheek. How abrasive. How presumptuous.

He talked to her about a bad storm, which swept through Maryland. She told him she had made out okay by staying put in the house until it passed.

He said it took him three hours to shovel the snow from his driveway. In the mist of the conversation his sister came over and said she needed him for a minute. He said "I'll talk to you later." He walked away. He never asked for her number.

How unusual. How peculiar. *How so different from Kweisii, he was not even willing to go out on a date with a woman. He had to be out right gay. No bisexuality. Or maybe his lover is near and maybe his lover is married and refuse to let Wayne date. His lover must be possessive. Who is he? Where is he?*

Alyson looked around the church. She noticed a man talking to Wayne. The same man who came up when they were talking the previous Sunday. *Is it him?*

The man talking to Wayne was Caucasian, short and bald with a flaccid stomach, just like Kweisii he could have done better. But Alyson knew this man's wife. *Did she know?*

It was obvious Wayne's family was active in his gay cover up. His sister intervened at the right moment. His mother gave him to front to keep women away.

But why hide in the church? Alyson decided to ride this one out. She had no real emotional investment in this man.

Nothing he could do would hurt her like Kweisii had. She had loved Kweisii with all her might. What she felt for Kweisii she had never felt for a man before and hereafter. Their souls touched.

Alyson believed in the truth. The truth would set Alyson free and hopefully the Peace Semble Church as well.

The devil had snuck in. His aim was to destroy. No church would be successful, in God's point of view, with a gay man as a deacon. God don't work that way.

Wayne was the abominable gay man in the Semble of God. Alyson was dishearten. *Here I go again.*

The next Sunday, Wayne and Alyson again found themselves sitting next to each other. This time at Wayne's bequest.

After service Alyson and Wayne stood to exist the church but they made yet another contact and Wayne did the hand sake and kiss again. But this time Alyson did not turn away. She had decided to put it all out there. In order to force him to retreat or commit.

If they at least had one long conversation she would discover the truth. She had nothing to lose. She already lost everything. She would never love another.

Wayne talked to her about her nostalgic behavior in the service. He knew something was different. What did he notice? That Alyson was vulnerable and easy to deceive. She must prove him wrong. The ball was in her hands.

Wayne walked with her to the exit door and at the right moment to connect, he pretended he spotted someone he needed to talk to and shouted, "Wait!" Then he fled away.

Alyson laughed. "That faggot."

When it all was over, after the revelation was revealed, then and only then would Alyson have anymore discussions with Crystal and Maria. They had too much faith in men.

Their experiences in life had been difference from hers.

♥♥♥♥♥

The game was over for

Alyson but not Wayne. He continued to flirt.

It wasn't Alyson he was flirting with but the leadership at Peace Semble Church. He was flirting with their spiritual awareness or lack thereof.

They were blinded by kindness. They should have been looking at things through the eyes of Jesus. When the rich man came to Jesus and said, "What can I do to be save?" Jesus knew his material things were his god so he said, "Sell all that you have." The man walked away sadly.

Why? Because Jesus saw the game. He wanted salvation; but he wanted it his way.

Wayne and Kweisii wanted salvation but they wanted it their way. We have to forsake all to follow Jesus.

It makes her angry that they believed others have to abandon anything that separates them from God but not them. Oh no they can keep their homosexual acts. "Don't be deceived. God is not mocked. Whatsoever a man sowed that she he also reap."

Alyson prayed she lived to see Wayne and Kweisii's reaping time. Wayne was an amateur.

Alyson contacted Pastor McCoy via email and informed him Wayne was gay and playing a game with her to convince the leaders of the church otherwise.

This was something she would have never done with the N.A.C.P. She would have never contacted, Mr.

Bind, Chairman of the N.A.C.P. and told him of Kweisii's game. They were not spiritual enough to seek out the truth, so she thought. How wrong she was.

She also mailed the Pastor a copy of her book *N.A.C.P. II National Association of the Collard Pew* to let him know she was speaking from experience not paranoia. She was well aware of the signs.

Unlike most women, her denial had died slowly and her reality had hit hard. She was not willing to play this game any further the female always loses. The cat was out the bag.

Alyson thanked God for her deliverance and she believed that Wayne would stay out of her face or she would slap him in his and was praying that he and Kweisii rot in hell. They say in hell the very thing that kept individuals from living for God on earth would be the thing eternally in front of their eyes in hell tormenting, but out of reach.

Alyson imagined Wayne and Kweisii in hell with men penises or buttocks constantly in front of them and the both of them desiring to have what they desired on earth so strongly, but being tormented because the very thing that separated them from God is ever before them but out of reach. Alyson was relieved that this would be their eternal fate.

Pastor McCoy outright rejected Alyson's email to her surprise.

It was apparent by what happened the next Sunday's morning service.

He gave out a man of the year award and Wayne was the recipient. The Pastor mocked Alyson. But why?

He said he had known Wayne for eight years and he had always been in agreement with him and he had never had any problems with him.

Alyson had attended this church for the past five years. He only knew Wayne three more years than Alyson. *So you're his lover. Oh my God!*

Alyson least expected the Pastor. The Bible says "There is a way that seem right to man but the end thereof is destruction."

Alyson had thought the Pastor was on the up and up. Not anymore. Wayne and Pastor McCoy was trying to get her to leave the church by mocking her every chance they got.

She wanted to jump up and run but running was not in her nature anymore.

She would stay a little while longer. She could not be the only one in the church reading the handwriting on the wall. "This man is gay and the Pastor maybe his lover."

Alyson attended the evening service purposefully, just to let the Pastor know *I'm not going anywhere. I'm going to stay right here until the truth is reveal. I'll be patient and watch you be dethrone. The time is near.*

That evening Peace Semble had a visiting Pastor, Pastor Brown, a black man, tall, medium weight and brawny, from Missouri.

He was promoting a mission trip to African in order to take medicine to AIDS victims. A worthy cause. Alyson would attend and donate a healthy offering.

When Pastor Brown stood up at the podium, Alyson caught a glimpse of Wayne. He froze. He was rigid.

Pastor Brown preached a sermon from Psalms twenty-four about God's sovereignty. "God is God and he is in control of us all. He can do what he wants when he wants and how he wants."

He seemed distracted by Wayne and his mother's presence. Pastor McCoy did not notice. He lacked wisdom.

Immediately following the service, Alyson noticed Pastor Brown motioning Pastor McCoy to his office. Wayne and his mother fled the scene. Alyson had never witnessed them leaving the church building so quickly.

Her instincts ventured. She decided to lay dormant longer than usual.

She held casual conversations with several women she had became friends with.

An hour had past and Pastor Brown and Pastor McCoy were still in Pastor McCoy's office. Alyson went home.

The next Sunday Alyson attended church on time. She had an antsy ness about her all week. When she arrived at the church, Wayne his mother, sister and daughter was not there. Unusual. But she thought they may have been running a little late. "Praise and Worship" service ended no Wayne or his family. The offering was taken, no Wayne nor his family. The soloist song before the pastor preached. No Wayne. Then Pastor McCoy began to preach.

He welcomed the district pastor to Peace Semble along with some other dignitaries. He had an important announcement to make to the church. Deacon Wayne Rivers would not be serving as deacon of Peace Semble any longer. He had been asked to resign. He went no further.

He preached a tearful message about deception and about the love and forgiveness of God and man. The other dignitaries sat pensively.

After service Alyson approached a friend. She was informed that Pastor McCoy had found out from Pastor Brown, who was also a medical doctor, that Wayne and his family was members of his church fifteen years ago in Saint Louis, Missouri.

That Wayne's daughter when she was around eight years old got hit by a car and was rushed to Doctor Brown's hospital emergency room. She had lost a lot of blood. She needed a blood transfusion. The family donated blood, Wayne, his mother, and his sister.

During the examination of the blood it was discovered the Wayne's daughter was also his sister. That Wayne's mother was also his daughter's mother and grandmother.

Pastor Brown confronted Wayne and his mother about their incestuous relationship and they admitted that they were lovers.

A week later the daughter was released from the hospital and the Rivers family disappeared, until now.

Wayne and his mother are engaging in incest. It's possible. No one has seen an ex-wife, nor has Wayne mother ever talked about an ex-husband. Incest normally goes on for generation. It is a generational sin; maybe Wayne's grandfather is his father. He told me once he was from a small country place outside of Saint Louis, Missouri. I've heard stories all my life how backward far away country people sleep with relatives. Wayne mother is his lover. Yuck!.

Alyson was speechless. She contacted Crystal and Maria and informed them that Wayne was not gay but having an incestuous relationship with his mother. "Yuck!" Wayne and his mother beat all, so Alyson thought.

Alyson was flabbergasted by this revelation.

She was familiar with incest and its ramification but she had only counseled females who were molested by dad, brother or/and uncle. She was not as knowledgeable about the symptoms when it came to male and mother.

Months after the revelation of Wayne and his mother being lovers, Alyson realized that one day by experiencing so much in life, like Mom-Pearl, her grandmother, "no surprise would pass her eyes."

She thought she had heard and seen it all with Kweisii and Saul and Wayne and his mother, Sheila, the wicked witch from the west, grooming her son to be her lover. How sick.

♥♥♥♥♥

Detouring from a book

signing at the Convention Center in Pittsburgh, to Susquehanna, Pennsylvania, to attend a shoe demonstration at her close friend Ann cousin's house, Alyson discovered that Kweisii and Saul nor Wayne and Sheila could beat all things she had ever experience or seen.

The book signing in Pittsburgh had went extremely well. Alyson had made contact with several Marylanders during the Book Fair and each one had promised they would not vote for Kweisii during the democratic primary elections in Maryland on September twelfth.

Alyson was relieved. Kweisii had become too confident after the judge ruled in his favor the first trial.

The second one would prove fatal to her if he won the senate seat.

Alyson's best friend Ann had attended the Pittsburgh Book Fair with Alyson.

She and Alyson were best friends at Temple. But when Alyson moved away to Columbia Ann and Alyson lost tract, getting caught up in marriage, children, and family. But Ann knew all Alyson's secrets and vice versa. She was there most of time when Alyson committed the crimes. Not too many.

Geraldo Rivera said that only five percent of Americans have a squeaky clean enough background to run for political office. And those who lacked the clean background should stop trying to pursue a political career.

For example, those with illegitimate children, or criminal

histories should leave the running for office to the five percent of clean Americans.

Alyson had not really committed crimes with Ann, in the true sense. When crimes are associated with Alyson, one would think of stalking a boyfriend, cutting boyfriend's tires, or putting sugar in his gas tank. Alyson may still qualify for a political office.

It was ironic how Ann and Alyson reunited. Alyson ran into Ann's mother at the hospital when she went in for her annual appointment to have a mammogram. Ann's mother was the reception. Alyson discovered that she and Ann only lived fifteen miles away from each other. The friendship quickly rekindled.

Ann dark and slim, poise and professional, always. She was always the calm thinker and Alyson the boastful reactor.

The ride to Pittsburgh was fun. Of course, they found local malls, shopping was one thing they always enjoyed together.

Maria was not much of a shopper.

While sitting in Ann's cousin's row house with a brick porch, in Susquehanna Alyson shared with Kathy, Ann's cousin, that her family visited a church in the area.

She did not know the name of the church but she knew the pastor's name was Texas. Kathy said the church was on the corner, down the street from her house.

Alyson was dressed in Capri's and t-shirt but she had missed several Sunday services and was driven to attend the service. "Go down the

street to the corner and turn right."
Ann did not want to go to church.

So alone Alyson walked the
paved block in Susquehanna, admiring
the row houses and how much they
resembled houses in Philadelphia.
She thought she had obeyed Kathy's
instructions.

There were several churches at
the corner on Central Street. *Which
one?*

Alyson noticed a young man
parking his Benz. He was very
attractive, light skinned, six feet tall
and dimples pressed in his cheek. He
spotted Alyson and smiled.

Alyson thought it was wise to
follow him into the church so she did.
She sat in the church for almost an
hour before asking the usher where
was Pastor Texas. "His church is

down the street." *Wrong church. Should I stay or go?*

Alyson decided to follow her initial plans and find Pastor Texas church.

Alyson left the wrong church and walk a half-block down to the right church. *I should have went left.*

Pastor Texas' church was charismatic. It was similar to her childhood church and her family's church in Philadelphia. Alyson no longer embraced the charismatic faith in the "old fashion" sense, the falling out on the floor, or the jumping and running around the church, the foaming at the mouth, or the inappropriate screeching screams.

Even as a child she felt bewildered by all this external display and had even known saints and minister who in spite of the show were not truly living a Christian life.

Alyson was not a perpetrator. She loved the Lord and had no problems raising her arms in worship and speaking praises to God. "I love you Lord," "Thank you Jesus."

But she was a little bit more reserve as a child and even as an adult. She did not knock people who praise God in that manner. She was just "different." Subsequently, searching for hope and deliverance she attended this church.

Alyson was slightly familiar with this Pastor from the Ameleke Convention. The name of the Annual Convention her family church umbrella under along with Pastor Texas church.

Alyson relaxed in the back row of the church. She had gotten there a little too late. Pastor Texas was rapping up his sermon.

After his sermon he made an altar call and many individuals went up seeking deliverance and healing. Thus the mayhem infested.

People were falling all over the floor and foaming at the mouth. Alyson was not unfamiliar with this form of surrender but it just seemed odd to her that the people lacked advancement and growth.

We were suppose to grow wicker but wiser. Where was the wiser?

While Alyson sat trying not to reveal what was pressing in her mind, settling in, Pastor Alexander Texas came around and stood in front of her. Her heart began pounding louder than the sound of the drums.

He said uncontrollably. "I know you. Have you ever been here before?"

She was taken aback. She whispered. "No."

He took the mike from his mouth and bent down and whispered in her ear. "Don't I know you?"

She whispered back. "Yeah. Charles." Before she could finish, he stood up and put the mike to his mouth. "I know this young lady. This is her first time here." He looked back at Alyson. "May I pray for you? The Lord is leading me to pray for you."

Alyson nodded and held her head down expecting him to lay a hand on her forehead and pray for her.

Instead he said. "Can you stand up?"

Stand up! What? Why? Cannot you see I have Capri's and a t-shirt on. Why draw attention to me? I'm not dressed in a suit with the brimmed hat and white pumps. My hair is jelled down and in a ponytail. I just wanted to get a little word in me and call it a day. Why are you putting me on the spot?

Alyson reluctantly obeyed. She stood up slowly.

He continued his banter. "I'm putting you on the spot aren't I?"

Alyson shyly responded. "Yes." She wanted to scream. Please stop!

He laughed and said. "Well, you are officially put on the spot."

Is this what this is a joke? Why is the joke on me? I just wanted to hear the word of God, not feel humiliation crashing down on me.

He was a single Pastor, with an ex-wife, which no one had ever seen or met, whose wife supposedly left him ten years prior for another man and moved to Jamaica. He had not dated since because he apparently was continuing to heal.

Alyson wondered if it would take her that long. She sympathized with him.

He began to prophesy to Alyson" The Holy Spirit sent you here!" He was shouting.

Alyson looked bewildered.

He repeated himself. "The Holy Spirit sent you here!" *Okay already.*

Alyson nodded in agreement. *Wonder why?*

He continued with authority. "The Holy Spirit sent you here, because you have needs. I have needs, and they have needs."

Don't we all have needs? How general.

Pastor Texas called a mother of the church over and asked her to pray for Alyson.

She did what he said but was less abrasive. She had a softer tone and was polite.

She whispered things in Alyson's ear, "You have a lot of gifts inside you. But you are afraid to use them. You need to let go and let God use your gifts. Stop running from what God has called you to do. I don't have to tell you this God has already told you. You have the gift to work with children. You are an excellent singer. Open you mouth and stop being ashamed to let God use you."

What she said Alyson had already heard many times before. She had the gift of seeing things.

Where was this gift the many years she yielding her heart to Key, her flesh to Kweisii, and her mind to Key culturing shocking her?

However, Alyson and the mother's spirits connected. Alyson had a feeling she knew the game.

At the end of the prayer, Alyson hugged her and thanked her for praying for her.

This was what Alyson had become accustomed too. But for Pastor Texas the hug wasn't enough. He wanted more outward showings.

Pastor Texas chimed in." I'm going to make you jump."

Alyson was thinking, *what in the world is going on here? I'm not jumping for anybody.*

Again the Pastor realizing Alyson was uncomfortable, laughed and said. "You won't have to jump by yourself. They" pointing to the audience, "will jump with you."

Alyson motioned the audience and they all nodded and shouted, "Yes, okay."

Pastor Texas obviously had the power over these people who were willing to do whatever he told them. Wow! Alyson had witnessed this power before.

"On the count of three you will jump three times. But let me move out the way because after the third jump the spirit is going to hit you and you will run all over this church."

Alyson glared in amusement, believing this was an intentional weird request considering this was her first time in attendance at this church.

He and others were okay with what was going on. He was persistent. He spoke louder in the microphone. "Let me move back because after she jump three times the spirit is going to fall all over her and she is going to run around this church."

Alyson tried to remain expressionless. She had no intentions of running around that church or any other church. She never had and was not about to start. Alyson jumped three times and went to her seat. The Pastor was angry.

Pastor Texas became indignant and preceded to talk to the audience as if Alyson was not there. "Some people have problems serving the Lord." Alyson was angry. *I have no problem serving the Lord. I have a problem with you trying to manipulate the Lord and me thinking you can control how I worship and praise God and how God chooses to use me.*

Again Alyson became presaged to the fact that something was amidst in this man's life and she wondered why his wife really left him. Had she really "backslid" turned her back on God and ran off with another man away in the beautiful island of Jamaica living happily ever after.

If such fate had befell her she was a lucky woman and God had shined on her, contrary to what Pastor Texas wanted people to believe. Alyson suppressed all other thoughts.

Weeks later after Alyson's visit to Pastor Texas church in Susquehanna; the Ameleke Convention was drawing nigh in Philadelphia.

Curiosity took over. What was really up with those Ameleke Pastors? Alyson felt safe to attend the night her cousin was preaching.

The Ameleke Convention was held every year for the past ten years in various states, Florida, Georgia, Maryland, Missouri, Connecticut, and Virginia. That year it was held in Philadelphia.

Alyson had attended one of the conventions in Miami, Florida five years prior.

Her church attendance was sporadic.

She spent most of the time going to the mall and to dinner with a college friend, who was, like Alyson experiencing a divorce, but unlike Alyson hers was taking a tremendous toll on her. Her driving was erratic. By the grace of God they barely escaped three car accidents.

Alyson's friend Stacey was rambling on and on. Alyson sense signs of depression but suppressed the urge in her to recommend professional counseling. Stacey had her Master's in

Counseling she knew the signs of depression.

The signs of depression are so concrete any professional should know them right away.

Alyson rambled on and on about Kweisii. But at that time it seemed so unfair that Alyson had found true love. Someone to grow old with but forever remain young in each other's eyes, while Stacey was on the verge of a nervous breakdown.

Nothing could quench Alyson's joy.

The Ameleke Convention was young and Alyson saw a lot of potential success for its spiritual and financial growth.

The ministers whose churches made up the body, on the surface, seemed sincere and honest. Anyway, if anything was fishy or unusual

Alyson was not in a position to notice. She was caught up in the reverie of what she thought could have been between her and Kweisii. Alyson had no reason, at the time, to think otherwise.

Alyson decided to attend the Ameleke Convention in Philadelphia, a few weeks after visiting Pastor Texas church in Susquehanna, with Sherry, her tall and lean sister, built like a run way model. She needed to start anew.

She had visited the church in Susquehanna. There were some whimsical occurrences but maybe it was her. Maybe she had lost her faith in man. She wanted to be proven wrong.

Pastor Texas had became of interest to Alyson. She had attended his church expected to get build up on the word, instead what she found left her mind boggled and confused. She needed answers. A wondering mind wanted to know.

Alyson attended a service and a banquet with Sherry on the Thursday's evening, her cousin was the guest preacher.

Alyson was aware that a lot of girls had crushes on Pastor Texas to know default of their own. He was relatively attractive, dark brown skin, Jamaican style, tall six foot two inches, slim with curling eyelashes, wide eyes and full lips, however he was soft.

Alyson had learned to move beyond outward appearances. Kweisii was superfine, sexy and very masculine.

People had to be assessed individually. What Alyson also knew was that Pastor Texas for the past ten years had not found one of the girls attractive or interesting enough to date.

While Alyson sat at the banquet enjoying her delicious soul food, macaroni and cheese, fried chicken, collards, foods she did not eat that often, mainly because she did not know how to cook them herself, and in addition, the restaurants in her area, along the Chesapeake Bay focused on cuisine food.

With a mouth full of macaroni and cheese, Alyson sat at the table with her mouth opened, speechless.

Sherry said out loud, "What is wrong with you?"

Alyson could only mustard up, "Look."

Low and behold Pastor Texas entered the banquet hall and walking by his side was a woman or was it?

The entire night Alyson studied the figure. The ankles were too wide. The legs too muscular. The hands were hidden. The features of the face were covered with thick-caked make up, clown style makeup. The figure was dark but the foundation was light. It thought light skinned women looked better than dark skinned women. The foundation circled the face like a clown's white paint. The weave, synthetic hair, hung to the buttocks wild and untamed.

One light of a match and it all would go up in flames. Just like Alyson thought the Pastor's career as a minister was going. The contacts were colored green. The breast were too pointy. A white scarf was tied around the neck to hide the Adam's apple. The clued eyelashes were clued too far up on the eyelid. Each eye had two sets of eyelashes.

It did not normally dress drag. Evident by the lack of skills in applying female miscellaneous.

It probably was a male in the service Alyson attended in Susquehanna. It never spoke. This was no woman. A transvestite.

The Pastor had brought a transvestite to church with him. Why?

Alyson suspected she had once again pressed the panic bottom. Could this be the man who followed her around the church after the service in Susquehanna?

It was this one particular man who trailed Alyson whereabouts after the service.

Alyson had thought he was flirting, but maybe she had got it wrong again.

This man felt threatened by her presence.

Alyson thought it was odd the Pastor never made eye contact with her and the man stood too close for comfort when she tried to explain to the Pastor that she was Charles' cousin.

The man even escorted her out the door. But he wasn't polite.

Alyson felt as if he was nonverbally saying "Get the hell out of here!"

He had to come dress drag. The other women were no threat. But Alyson she was a threat.

They believed if the Pastor failed to connect with her then people would wonder why.

They comprised a planned. The Pastor had to make the members of Ameleke think he already had a woman. "Throw on this dress and make-up and lets get out of here."

If he was use to dressing drag he would have done a better job. Anyone would know that.

Alyson was able to put it all together. His wife had found out he was gay. She flipped. And he put out that she was "crazy" just in case she told the truth one day.

Unlike Alyson, she was not vibration and the fight was not in her. She would walk through the world wounded and never overcoming the deception.

How brassy of this Pastor. He must really believe he had the people wrapped around his finger. Did he? Yes he did.

♥

At the banquet table, Alyson tried to whisper to her sister and mom that the so called woman with Pastor Texas was a man.

Her sister refused to observe the ankles. Her mother said Alyson was bringing down a man of God and she would have no part.

It was incredulous for them. They did not share the experiences Alyson had.

They were indomitable to the belief system that this Pastor was a holy and righteous man. They lacked the conformity of the truth.

Initially, the Pastor sat with pseudo confidence.

Consequently, Alyson believed her unadulterated stares set him off line. He was quite nervous. He had no need to be. He had the power.

He and the other Pastors, who probably had their own dark secrets, had compiled a group of ignorant, unrighteous people, who had taken on the form of righteousness but were denying the power of God and the direct word of God, which specifically say homosexuality was an abomination and sin.

Alyson was overwhelmed during the ride home. How could her family accept such behavior and not take flight and flee?

She had always thought they were too religious, but lacked spirituality. "Having a form of godliness but denying the power of God."

They had a lot of jealousy. They did a lot of backstabbing. They failed to rejoice with those who rejoiced and they often rejoiced when others wept.

They wept when others had something to rejoice about.

But how far away from the Lord had they traveled to accept the ultimate deception of the devil?

Alyson had to sum up the pastor bringing a transvestite to church won the prize.

It beat incest, and Saul and Kweisii's deceptive relationship. She had seen it all. Or had see?

Pastor Texas was a nice looking man What a waste. Alyson noted that some people focus as a *nearsighted child*, only capable of seeing the pain and hurt in front of them, leaving the joy of life in the far distance as a blur.

Alyson and Crystal summed up that most incest family members touch inappropriately in public because they struggle with what's appropriate and what's not.

What we see as inappropriate they see as okay because their inappropriateness goes well beyond the human eye and the "normal" human mind.

Crystal said as far as the pastor goes, "let us just say he's not a pastor."

The possibility of Wayne Rivers being a gay deacon meant nothing at all to Alyson and did not throw her into therapy. She only regretted that a man who physical resembled Idris Alba, the preacher in the movie *The Gospel*, the sexy actor in *Sometimes in April* and the hunk from *The Wire* could be anything put "normal" and "straight."

Alyson's encounters with Wayne were brief and her suspicion was from the onset.

♥

She subconsciously analyzed that if Wayne really liked her, or was interested in her, in spite of her non-reactions, most men would take a leap of faith and try and communicate and date the woman anyway, with exceptions to brothers on the down low.

They tend to cut potential relationships prematurely short.

Alyson was aware that there were down low brothers like Kweisii who engaged in sex in order to pretend to be heterosexuals, by engaging in bisexuality, to cover up their homosexuality.

But Wayne was just gay, at least in Alyson's mind, until she found out otherwise.

She lacked experience and knowledge with men who were engaging in incest with their mothers, so she was, as Crystal put it, "confusing the symptoms of brother on the down low with incest behavior."

There was a reason for his open flirtations and private retreats Alyson was aware of that fact; but lacked the knowledge of the reasoning.

Alyson would find herself seeking another church home. She had no other choice but to accept that the leaders of this church lacked wisdom and knowledge and were not as spiritual as they appeared.

How could this man sit under their leadership for so many years and they not question his relationship with his mother.

From what Alyson saw things were pretty bizarre. She just thought he was using his mother to keep women away. But the leadership had witness way more interactions than Alyson yet they behaved as if everything was okay and even tried to force Alyson and some other members to look at the situation with *eyes wide shut.*

Alyson recalled a morning service. An altar call was made after the preaching. Wayne and his mother made their way to the altar. His mother kneeled closely beside him and he hugged her around her waist. The entire section

Alyson was sitting in watched intently. The pastor took notice. He made a statement "don't be distracted by what is going on up here. Think about what you need."

But Alyson and others were distracted. Distracted to the point that they wonder why he was allowing such behavior to take place and giving the devil the power to distract others from concentrating on the Lord.

Alyson imagined he was one of those type individuals who pretended everything was okay when things were quite the contrary.

Individuals who function in this denial state were normally children who had been molested, came from abusive homes, or/and had an addictive parent or parents.

Alyson did not know enough about this man's background to assess any further.

What she did know was if he had been preaching for forty years, as he claimed, then he should have known from experience how to "nip things in the bud."

Why was he reluctant to call Wayne and his mother into his office and request that they stop the inappropriate touching?

He could simply say "it just don't look right."

Contrary, he was asking the church to pretend it wasn't happening. What was in this man's closet?

Alyson felt it best to leave before she became just as sick as all the individuals who had sat in that church for years and accepted this incest.

Alyson did not believe when Pastor Brown revealed to Pastor McCoy that Wayne and his mother were lovers that he had no clue. He was just forced to take action because he was not sure who else Pastor Brown would tell this information too.

Alyson was like most women in their forties who were single, she was lonely. She hoped and prayed for someone to love and spend the rest of her life with, enjoying nature and taking long walks in the park, and holding hands at the movies. Wayne may have brought that relief. She was willing to give him a chance. She should have known better.

♥♥♥♥♥

Alyson sat at her home on a Friday night watching Miami Heat Professional Basketball team playing against the New Jersey Nets.

She had an interest in the Heat because of Alonzo Mourning's life story. He was playing for the Heat a second time.

She wanted him to get a championship and then maybe he'll retire. He was playing after receiving a kidney transplant.

Alyson would have donated one of her kidneys but she was no match. Playing professional basketball was risky. But he did not seem to care.

He played with all the aggression, finesse, and zeal he played with prior to his kidney transplant.

Alonzo was a foster care child who volunteering offered to go into foster care because he was not satisfied with is home life. It was the right decision. God had a plan and he was wise enough to vision it. He was placed in the right foster home in which his talents could be festered. He was chosen to play basketball for Georgetown University then onto Professional Basketball. A success story.

Alyson wondered if he had a "bearly friend" to tell all his troubles too.

Alyson also had an interest in Vince Carter who played basketball for the New Jersey Nets, not the same interest she had in Alonzo Mourning. Her son Mitoses and Vince were twins. The resemblance, voice tone, physiognomy, facial expressions, and mannerism were so identical. That was eerie. Were they really brothers?

♥

Alyson sat engaging in the antics of the game of professional basketball, reminiscing to a better time in her life, when the telephone rung with annoyance.

The game was tied and the New Jersey Nets were matching Miami Heat's shots score for score.

If only Richard Jefferson would accept that Vince Carter was their Mariano Rivera, their closer, then the Nets could beat the Miami Heat. But no such luck Miami was surging and Richard Jefferson were taking uncontested shots and missing. He wanted to be the closer. God had not chosen them.

If Vince Carter was only a little more aggressive and demanding, a little Michael Jordan arrogant should emerge with him, and then the New

Jersey Nets could be more successful in the playoff.

Instead, Alyson imagined a young attractive man, who had other men player hating on him throughout his life, so he decided to compromise for peace sake.

Alyson conceded the Nets would lose the series so why not answer the telephone.

On the fourth ring she picked up the telephone, reluctantly saying "hello."

To Alyson's surprise it was Dr. Ruiz. He was checking up on her to see how she was doing. He wanted to know if she was ready for another trial. The trial in Virginia was nearing. Carll was free forever.

Alyson was surprise to here from Dr. Ruiz. It was nice to talk with him again. His voice brought her relief.

♥

"Yeah. I'm up to it. I have to be." Alyson took a couple of deep breaths.

"I know. I'm sorry about what happened in Baltimore. That sucks." He said sympathetically.

"Yeah. But I'm not surprised. Baltimore is so corrupt. Maybe now that the media is digging into how he possible got off 'scot free'——all the corruption will come to a head."

"Maybe Baltimore went a little too far with its nepotism this time. Maybe they should have at least given him probation, or a certain length of time. Something."

"That would have been feasible. But the judge wanted to make people believe the jurors error and Kweisii is innocent. You see he did not withdraw his run for senate. The only thing I say is Kweisii is sleeping or have had sex with the right men."

Dr. Germaine Ruiz laughed and said, "Yuck! That's nasty."

Alyson found herself laughing too. She was suspicious of all men but maybe Dr. Ruiz was not gay?

Alyson continued. "That is the only way I can sum up what has taken place. It could not all be about his power as ex-president and chief executive officer of the National Association of the Collard Pew. I believe a lot of powerful men have a lot to hide and Kweisii know what they are hiding."

"Well, hopefully he does not have anything negative on the men in politics in Virginia. So maybe you can get a fair trail here."

"That is if he doesn't win the senate seat prior to the trial. I don't have any faith in the state of Virginia. Why do you think the judge ordered

♥

the trial date around the same time as the senate election in Maryland? Virginia is probably corrupt too. I don't think any state in the United States avoids political corruption."

"Wow! What happened to that optimistic young lady I discharged from the hospital?"

Life, circumstances and time have worn her down. Alyson sounded depressed. She wanted to shake off the depression.

Dr. Ruiz did not deserve to witness that side of her but she was powerless. She would never tell him about Chip and Wayne.

She was beginning to believe that something was seriously amidst with her to be attracting so many creeps.

She wondered why she was finding these men and what she could do to change the outcome? *What is wrong with Dr. Ruiz? Is he gay? Did Kweisii pay him to call me and find out something negative about me to bring to trial? Kweisii had been successful squashing my hopes and dreams. He had won. He did not need to send anyone else into my life. He could throw his hands up in victory. He had knocked me out, temporarily. I would not let Dr. Ruiz in or any other man. I could never trust and love again.*

Alyson paused a long time. Dr. Ruiz patiently waiting for a response.

"Men, men have turned me into a pessimistic person. Justice. It's hard to accept justice is not blind. God. It's difficult to accept that God has failed to protect me."

"I guess I can understand why you're so sultry. You have been through a lot. More experiences than two women in a lifetime. But I'm quite sure God won't put any more on you than you can bear." He laughed. "I'm not too spiritual. Isn't that how the scripture goes?"

Alyson retorted. "Something like that."

Alyson knew he had quoted part of the scripture verbatim. Why was Dr. Ruiz quoting scriptures from the Bible?

Chip had come quoting scriptures. Jehovah Witness style and twisted. He had her fooled for a while.

Maybe he was trying to encourage her or maybe he was coming the way Chip had come, knowing more about her than she had let on. Chip said he was good at reading people. Lies. All lies.

Chip was so good that eventually Alyson let her guard down and told him were she lived. He came to visit several times.

They snuggled on the couch and watched movies and ate pizza and nipped on popcorn. He told jokes and Alyson laughed. Alyson told jokes and he laughed.

They made plans for the future. Alyson suppressed how much he favorite Kweisii. He was short and bow legged, a little lighter that Kweisii. His smile lid up his face. His eyes sparkled.

The sparkled had left from the man who sat in the front passenger seat the day Alyson was dragged in the black Escalade. It was Chip. He was timid and spoke passively. "Man you said you only wanted to talk." But doing the trial he pleaded the fifth. There was no connecting him or Kweisii's son to the crime scene. His loyalty was to his blood relative not a woman he had toyed with for months.

Dr. Ruiz quoted scripture but Alyson did not want to hear scripture. Nor did she want him trying to encourage or patronize her whichever was which. She wanted no advice.

She did not want anyone telling her to trust and believe in love. She was not as lucky as Kweisii.

He had found Carll early and they had spent twenty-five years together before she came on the scene. No way she could have broken that bond.

Dr. Ruiz was no different from the rest. I'll dare him. After the Virginia trial, whatever the outcome, he'll vanish like an owl in the day.

"I'm glad you understand." Alyson said nonchalantly.

"How about we change the course of this conversation. I'm going to be in your area next week at a training at John Hopkins University Hospital do you want to hook up and go to dinner. I hear there's some nice restaurants in Saint Michael's. Are you from Saint Michaels?"

Alyson became freighted. He must know were she lived and that she was only sixty miles from Saint Michaels. When the conversation end she would contact her friend who own a log cabin near Rehoboth Beach and move down there, again. She would not take any more changes. The risk was deadly. *I better play it cool.*

Dr. Ruiz continued. "Well, if Baltimore is too painful for you maybe we could go to a restaurant up your way. I know there are nice restaurants along the Chesapeake Bay.

We can even go into Delaware if you're like that better. I really want to see you, Alyson."

The sound of her name was piercing like a tattoo being carved into her skin but romantically and whimsical. *Why?* Her heart melted. Dr. Ruiz was persistent.

She at one point believed he was honest and sincere. Now she was ambivalent.

The recent experiences of the past was hunting. Her heart was ax down and fell silent like a tree in the forest with no one around to hear the crash.

She wondered what Kweisii had on Dr. Ruiz, which would make him play the game.

Maybe he had a sexual affair with his male roommate, like Scottie Pigeon. Maybe he had sex once with a minor patient. Or Maybe he had a fatal medical accident that the hospital covered up. Why was he so persistent? It had been a year. Why now?

It was unfathomable to believe that he had been thinking about her since he last saw her and was waiting for the right moment to have an excuse to contact her.

Dr. Ruiz had spent the last year making every attempt to forget Alyson. He felt it was not ethical for him to fall in love with an ex-patient, especially one so wounded, fragile, and lifeless. He believed it was not love but maybe infatuation or sympathy.

He always fell in love with strong and vibration women. Something Alyson no longer was. But yet he still longed for her. "Like the deer panted after the water."

Dr. Ruiz resented that his mother was so passive and never stood up to his dad. She was such a desperate housewife.

Every woman he tried dating mistakenly thought he wanted a replica of his mother after meeting her they changed.

They were trying to please him. They wanted him or a doctor at all cost.

He was not looking for a miniature Mrs. Venus Ruiz. She was a beautiful woman, short and slim but with wide hips, lips perky, cheeks wide and eyes narrowed and bright. Her black and straighten hair hung almost to her buttocks.

He resembled his father but his complexion was somewhere between his mother and father.

The women were phonies his mother was genuine.

As a child he wanted her to say, "yes" just sometimes when Daddy said "no." But that never happened.

Alyson would challenge him, the old Alyson would. How could he get her back to that person? It was his civil duty.

As Alyson recovered at the hospital she was different from all women he had met.

She was not moved by his money or position or physiognomy. Most of his female patients made excuses to continue to contact him after being discharge from the hospital married and single.

Alyson said, "Thank you" and went home and he never heard from her again until he saw her in the courtroom in Baltimore.

After the trial again she said "Thank you," and went home. He expected her to be like the rest. He kept his cellular telephone near, even when he should have locked it into his locker at the hospital. At home he stayed near the telephone. She never called.

Germaine recalled how, in Baltimore, elated he was to receive the subpoena to testify in the trial. He thought she would be just as happy to see him.

He made sure he wore his best suit, beige Calvin Klein with black leather shoes and dark brown tie. She had shared with him in the hospital she loved fall colors.

The trial was held in the spring so he thought she would notice the fall colors and appreciate him for trying to please her.

When he was called to the stand, he walked by Alyson expecting a smile or a wink. She failed to focused on him.

He hoped beyond measure that her attorney told her to avoid eye contact with him so the jurors wouldn't think she was influencing him or swaying his testimony in her favor.

But after the court session he saw her in the corridor and again she just said, "Thank you." She quickly exited the courthouse. He had thought they connected in the hospital. She remembered him brushing her hair. He left the Baltimore courtroom despondent.

While riding home, that day, after he testified in Baltimore, he reflected on the courtroom stand, but in spite all the medical questions he responded to the only thing he recalled was how he unsuccessfully struggled to make eye contact with the attorney questioning or interrogating him and not Alyson.

He was being drawn into Alyson by chemicals bonds not yet discovered by man.

Every time he focused on her she stared expressionless. He caught the eye of Kweisii and for some reason his heart skipped a beat with freight. Mr. Mfumey glared at him with those daring eyes dressed in his Armani suit, as if he could read the love for Alyson in his heart. Yet he gloated over the fact, unconsciously, that she would never love another as much as she had loved him.

Dr. Ruiz had a lot of work ahead of him. If he believed in love, he could tell Alyson was apprehensive about his call.

He felt the drive to explain to her how much he loved her and how it was impossible for him to get her off his mind, but Alyson said quickly "Call me when you get into Baltimore. I'll see. I have to go now. Talk soon." The telephone went silent.

♥♥♥♥♥

Alyson was still unemployed and she wondered if employment would ever come to greet her again. It had to come soon.

Tazzy would be eighteen in four years. Her father would not at that point feel obligated to maintain a certain lifestyle for Tazzy; therefore, she reaping the benefits.

Tazzy's spirit remained as bright as the sunrise. Nothing could shake her.

Alyson envied her confidence. She had a sympathy and passion for others that had long left Alyson. This was evident by an event Alyson and Tazzy attended in Baltimore.

Alyson and Tazzy attending the African American Festival one bright July afternoon.

Alyson knew it would be risky because Kweisii frequently made appearance at these events soliciting votes. But her life had been on hold long enough.

Sure as the sky was blue Alyson and Tazzy ran directly into Key's path. The path was dark and gloomy. He had to his side, caressing hands gently, a fcmale, another one chosen to cover up his homosexuality, but as Alyson studied the individual further she realized Pastor Texas was not the only one flaunting a he/she. Saul was dressed up like a woman.

She had often wondered which one played which role, now she painfully knew, Key was the man and Saul the woman. How confusing.

Kweisii knew the people in Baltimore were content with his

sexuality and rightfully so, it was his life not theirs.

Alyson may have felt the same if she had not been a victim of his past in which she could not escape in the future.

Tazzy, like the people in Baltimore, could not understand why her mother could not just accept Kweisii, her Key, was gay and go on, without resolution. He was found "not-guilty" maybe it really wasn't him.

The dagger had been removed. The bleeding was stopped so let the wound heal. Easier said than done.

Key and Tazzy embraced and they were very friendly and cordial to one another. Alyson stood motionless.

She wanted Tazzy to hate him as much as she did. But longing to be a true born again believer in Jesus

Christ she knew she could not teach her children or grandchildren to be unforgiving and to hate, even if she, at that moment, struggled with those character flaws.

So she sat in her folding chair and allowed Tazzy to enjoy the evening playing and socializing with Key's grandchildren, nieces and nephews, as if all was really quiet on the *western front.*

Alyson felt pessimistic about the pending trial in Virginia. She knew of the power of nepotism in America. While playing the game of life with Kweisii she could just whisper "I want" and she got. Now the tables were turned. She shouted "I need!" The response was "so what."

In spite of David's quote in Psalms "I once was young but now

I'm old, but I've never seen the righteous forsaken nor his seed begging bread,"

Alyson gazed for longing. For she no longer had to wonder how far would Kweisii go to get his revenge.

Any man who would beat and rape her, made it apparent he would have no problems create a world for her in which homeless lurked at any given moment, but the outcome remained to be seen.

Who really had the power the self-preservation Kweisii or the loving God, or did the New Age have it right that the power lies within us that we are our own gods? Was Alyson failing to tap into the power of the god within her?

———

Alyson had been without need then in need then without need then back in need and without need now in need.

Her stability in life has been like a roller coaster ride. Being borne into an American Middle Class African American family with two working parents, she was often without need. Then her parent's separated and she was in much need. Then several people were placed in her path and she was without need. Then they left and she was in need.

She had to conquer that demon which left her much in need, emotional, physically, and financially. The demon was winning in round five.

Alyson wasn't looking forward to the rape trial in Virginia. All hope was gone. But she could not back out

She really believed that Kweisii had tapped into his sources in Virginia and a similar trial to Baltimore's trial would be repeated. The redundancy of failure.

She would not walk away, she was unnerved, and Kweisii would win.

What frighten Alyson the most was whether or not Kweisii, once he conquered, would leave her alone or would he accept his prowess and finish what he started months ago. She could not see him letting her live. The odds were tilted. The faith in a God who protects was shattered.

Alyson was not a feline. Actually felines rejected her as their master. All her life she possessed cats and dogs.

Dogs were her favorite. Cats were tolerable. A week prior to the kidnapping her cat Daisy attacked her in a weird way.

It was the most unusual circumstance. She had attended a book signing at a retreat in Ocean City to promote *N.A.C.P. Notations Admix the Collard Pew,* her first book.

The book that made men close to her, men she had grew up with in the church, angry at her thus revealing their sexual preference. *Why would a straight guy be angry or reject a book a girl wrote about a gay guy. A man could write a thousand books about how to tell a woman is a lesbian, I could care less. Ladies beware. There are more down low brothers out there than you believe.* She returned home jubilant.

The book signing was a success and shopping was a joy.

People often say the Christmas season is the most wonderful time of the year. It really is. It is the most wonderful time of the year because in spite of Santa's naughty and nice list and in spite of all the fixtures around the house husbands has failed to work on because of the explosive of sports on television; there is an ideation of peace.

Life is full, beginning with the World Series opening up the holiday sports season.

Bring on the men with the perfect buttocks who are constantly fixing their jockey straps in public as if to say it cannot hold it.

Then onto football season. Bring on the men in tights with the perfect thighs and buttocks who wear their jockey straps without underwear.

Oh and don't forget the college bowls. Shortly after the college bowls the National Basketball Association gets all the attention it deserves. The belief is that football players are better looking than Basketball Players; however, basketball players tall and slimness gives them omnipotence over the football players.

In addition, to the husbands swallowing themselves in sports wives don't care because they get to shop and secretly lust after their favorite professional athlete. Is it Derek Jeter or Alex Rodriguez? Is it Kevin Garnett or Shaquille O'Neil? After all is said and done all can go to Christmas Eve service and ask for forgiveness of all wrong doings recognizing that Jesus' birth is the real reason for the season.

Everything would remain wonderful if husbands allowed their wives to shop all year long with no complaints.

It was the belief that wives complained because money is short and they cannot shop. Its often said "money don't bring happiness.

Look at the people in Hollywood, the stars, and their divorce rate and drug abuse."

But it goes without saying money brings relief. When a wife cannot shop the children's negative behavior is heighten, the husband's lazy, the house is a wreck and in disarray, the dog needs a bath, the cat litter needs to be change six times a day, and the hamster was a mouse that's why the cat ate it.

So therein Alyson found herself blissful from a book sighing and shopping.

At 12:30 a.m. carrying a handful of bags, she walked in the door and at the top of the stairs was Daisy, her domestic feline, glaring at her in an unusual manner.

She climbed up the stairs weary and just two steps shy of the top, she learned over to pat Daisy on the head when she leaped at Alyson like a "man-eating" lion worth a shortage of suitable food.

Alyson had became an easy prey instead of the hand that cuddled and fed her for the past three years. Alyson immediately threw up her bags as a safeguard and fled down the stairs. Just as she got to the front door, Daisy latched onto her and gnawed into her flesh while scratching her leg.

Alyson ran to her neighbor's house and with his permission; although his brother one third mile up the road hung a confederate flag on his doorpost, she called the SPCA. The

SPCA reluctantly came out to her home, because they don't normally come and get cats, and took Daisy away and put her to sleep.

Since Alyson had to pretend it was a neighbor's cat gone wild, in order for the SPCA to come and get her withered Daisy, Daisy's head was cut off and tested for Rabies. Alyson was sent to the emergency room to began preparations for Rabies treatment just in case her neighbor's wild cat had Rabies. Alyson knew better. The Rabies test came back negative, but not before Alyson received two shots of penicillin with the longest needles she had ever seen. See how far a lie can go.

Alyson did not weep for this pet as she did the animals that proceeded her in death.

Alyson has yet to understand the bizarreness and unnatural non-instinctive ness of Daisy's behavior.

If an animal that only function on instinctual behavior, which lacked the power of the will of human reasoning, could be so unpredictable, why would she expect Kweisii, with such power, to demonstrated any more controlled behavior. Alyson decided she would just take life one day at a time.

Alyson sat outside on her lanai. It was the midnight hour. She gazed into the sky.

It was May and Jupiter was at it closest to the earth. If she had a telescope she could view Jupiter cloud Belts, the Great Red Spot and Jupiter's four moons, Io, Europa, Granymede, and Callisto, circling the planet. If she was not so exhausted she would climb up in the attic find the telescope and study this planet.

It would be many years before it would come this close to earth again. Instead she would only observe the view made visible by the naked eye. The fact that Jupiter shines ten times brighter than any star around it made it easy to detect.

As quickly as she sat reminiscing about all the knowledge of the solar system obtained in Astronomy 101 her mind shifted to Dr. Germaine Ruiz. Why had he called? Was he really genuinely concerned about her? How could she know? Kweisii was so convincing, loveable and understanding. He fulfilled the desires of her heart. He fulfilled every desire of her life.

As she reflected back on her relationship with Kweisii she realized it was too good to be true. She laughed as she thought about Kweisii bugging her telephone line and then pretending to be so knowing. How could she be so stupid? "I like Aruba."

One summer she shared this with Maria. And low and behold Kweisii presented her with a surprise trip to Aruba for her fortieth birthday. She was in heaven. The sex was perfect. She had never shared with anyone what she preferred. How could he had fulfilled her so? Maybe because he felt they were one, female-on-female.

Dr. Ruiz was saying all the right words and was making all the right moves. His appearance at the court house in Baltimore during the trial was stunning. When he was rushed in to testify her heart skipped a beat.

He was dressed impeccable. His eyes sparkled. This frightened

Alyson.　　Her heart melted with sadness.

Germaine was a man searching for love and he was making every attempt to gravitate toward her.　But why?

Why would another man want to date her after knowing all the drama she had went though with Kweisii.

As intelligent as he was he should know she was scared for life. He should know her trust was shattered for eternity.

Why would he want a woman nagging him and questioning him about his every move especially when it came to his relationships with his male friends?　He had to have a hidden agenda.　Alyson would not be hurt again. She promised herself.

The night became breezy. The trees blew and bowed to God's command.

The clouds were slowly beginning to cry. The rain dripped on her head. She slowly and emphatically walked into the house, crawled under her goose blanket and after two hours of tossing and turning and fantasizing that some where some how she would find a man who was not gay or a bisexual and live happily ever after she fell asleep.

Although Dr. Ruiz's face was compiled of that man who dominated her fantasy, he was not the man with whom she could smell reality.

♥♥♥♥♥

The days were long and

dreadful, but peaceful. The trial was quickly approaching in Richmond, Virginia, so was the senate election. In Maryland, Kweisii had accused the Democratic Party of blind sitting him and favoring his opponent because they threw all their money his opponent's way.

He was not the promise child for the Democratic Party. They had close friends within the N.A.C.P. II, and they were aware of the books *Notations Admix the Collard Pew* and *National Association of the Collard Pew N.A.C.P. II*

Kweisii was trailing in the polls. The people in Maryland, the knowledgeable people in Maryland, understood that he was a self-absorbent asshole who had deceived them for years. The odds were stacked up against him.

In addition, the debacle with Senator Faley soliciting the young pagers on Capital Hill for sex had surface. And those association with the Collard Pew were aware that although Faley was a Republican and Kweisii a Democrat, that he had described Faley during a National Association of the Collard Pew Convention as a real good friend. Many wondered why out of all the men in White House Faley became his friend? The outcome of the election was detrimental to her.

Alyson could not escape the coldness of reality no matter how hard she tried. Tucked away assumingly safe in a prestigious hotel in Virginia, under an assumed name, watching the negativity of the world unfolding on

CNN. Who ever heard of a Tsunami? It was several days before the trial in Richmond.

Alyson received another telephone call from Dr. Ruiz. He wanted to shelter her from the storm. How did he know the storm was approaching? He was a doctor not a weather man. He offered to open the doors of his home to her but she preferred instead to stay in a hotel under an assumed name, Leah Marshall. Security would be near.

Alyson had normally visited Richmond as a vacation spot. She recalled a visit she made with Kweisii just two years prior, not too long ago. They resided at the Jefferson Hotel.

At that time Kweisii had an assumed name. They walked through the historic hotel with open hearts. The hotel, which opened in 1895, reflected the sensibilities of the age of their love.

The hotel once had separate parlors for men and women, Kweisii and Alyson had been separated by history and past, yet the replica of their love, like the antique replica furniture and faux-marble columns, had spruced up.

The Virginia Museum of Fine Arts was practically empty when she went there with Kweisii that vacation. What a treat.

They were able to cuddle and kiss without resolution or disgust from on lookers believing they should get a room.

They admired the ancient Indian art.

Considering most African-Americans have Indian blood somewhere in their DNA, there seem to be a connection but mainly with Kweisii. His Native American heritage and history had been past down from his family from generation-to-generation.

Alyson noticed, that day the red tin that embarked within his skin, giving him the glow of love and life that she longed for.

They strolled the James River walkway while holding hands as to never let go.

They plied the water on a narrated historic Richmond Canal Cruise floating in all the love that Alyson, at that time, believed God had bestowed upon them.

They ate at Julep's restaurant and for the first time Alyson took a taste of Vidure wine, while Kweisii recited poetry written by Poe, she did not believe in drinking alcohol, but with

Kweisii everything was anew, even the banana foster cheesecake with caramel topple.

The Edgar Allan Poe Museum Enchanted Garden was being considered for the wedding ceremony. The poetry of Edgar Allen Poe gripped both their hearts. She could still hear Kweisii's voice...

Oh! that my young life were a lasting dream!
My spirit not awakening, till the beam
Of an Eternity should bring the morrow.
Yes! tho' that long dream were of hopeless sorrow,
'Twere better than the cold reality
Of waking life, to him whose heart must be,
And hath been still, upon the lovely earth,

*A chaos of deep passion, from his
birth.
But should it be- that dream eternally
Continuing- as dreams have been to
me
In my young boyhood- should it thus
be given,
'Twere folly still to hope for higher
Heaven.
For I have revell'd, when the sun was
bright
I' the summer sky, in dreams of living
light
And loveliness,- have left my very
heart
In climes of my imagining, apart
From mine own home, with beings
that have been
Of mine own thought- what more
could I have seen?
'Twas once- and only once- and the
wild hour*

From my remembrance shall not pass-
some power
Or spell had bound me- 'twas the
chilly wind
Came o'er me in the night, and left
behind
Its image on my spirit- or the moon
Shone on my slumbers in her lofty
noon
Too coldly- or the stars- howe'er it
was
That dream was as that night-wind- let
it pass.

I have been happy, tho' in a dream.
I have been happy- and I love the
theme:
Dreams! in their vivid coloring of life,
As in that fleeting, shadowy, misty
strife
Of semblance with reality, which
brings

♥

To the delirious eye, more lovely things
Of Paradise and Love- and all our own!
Than young Hope in his sunniest hour hath known.

After Alyson's second night at the Richmond hotel under her assumed name, a luxurious hotel with hanging chandelier and a lobby, not a hotel you just walk up to the door. You had to travel into the lobby by revolving doors. Walk on the oriental blush rugs, no throw rugs, past the winged brown leather chairs and floral green and white love seats with the one hundred percent wooden end tables with gold lamps, pass the receptionist section where the women and men were dressed in navy blue

Armani suits with white cotton shirts and blue and white stripped necktie, women wearing skirts, men pants, pass the concierge, to the elevators which lead to all thirty floors with no number thirteen button and restaurant button for the above the building restaurant where the floors revolved and the view of Richmond lead to the Potomac River, the telephone rung. Alyson answered it.

On the other line was a lady a black female supposedly. She shouted, "You bitch! How much is the white man paying you to destroy the black man? First Clarence Thomas, O.J. Simpson, Michael Jackson and now Kweisii Mfumey! You Anitra Hill wanna bee! You whore!" She slammed the telephone down with a bang.

♥

Alyson's ocular vibrated within her eardrum. Alyson nervously hung up the telephone.

A few minutes later the telephone rung again. Alyson was reluctant to answer but it might be Tazzy or Mitose checking on her.

"Hello." She quietly said.

This time a black man spoke firmly and harshly. "You think you're going to get away with this! I'm watching you! And I know where you are! You cannot hide! You mother fucker!"

In the midst of hands trembling while hanging up the telephone, Alyson comically thought, in the midst of death, that if Kweisii had his cronies call her hotel room he had surely placed himself in some bad company, O.J. Simpson, Michael Jackson, *Oh boy what a loser.*

Alyson telephoned the hotel receptionist. "Can you please hold all calls and take messages for me?" The hotel receptionist agreed. One hour later the telephone rung again. Believing it must be a family member or the receptionist would have held the call for safekeeping, she answered confidently. It would be nice to hear a familiar voice. "Hello." No answer. "Hello."

The voice on the other line was shrill with laughter. Hysteria. Alyson slammed the telephone down. She needed rescuing.

She crept to the door and peeped through the peep hold. She would make the officer outside her door aware of her pending doom. She peeped through the peep hold. She saw no figure. She opened the door slightly. The officer was gone. She searched up and down the hallways. No one.

The only thing she could see or hear was a shadow and the exit door slowly and precisely closing. Nervously she picked up the telephone and dialed Dr. Germaine Ruiz's home number.

He was the only person she knew who could get to her quickly. She had to, at that moment, trust someone.

Dr. Ruiz did not answer the first impede call. His voice mail picked up. "Damn it!"

Alyson seldom cursed and did not think it was a good idea to be doing so.

If someone came in and killed her she wondered if God would spare her soul damnation in hell for her final words.

The inconvenience of voice mail. She remember the days, back in college, when she could call a cheating boyfriend and scream to the telephone answering machine while he was making love to another girl, "I know you're there. You no good lying dog. Is she with you now? That whore! She can have your sorry ass."

How she really did not mean the other woman could have him. She was into "ballers" and they were handsome and fine, tall and dark, bow legged, and rich.

In her final moments of life on earth her youth and innocent days flashed before her.

If she had only stuck to professional ball players she would be safe.

Why did she forsake what she knew? The days when she was so

beautiful that she had the attitude toward men, "You all come a dime a dozen."

She really could have another professional athlete in a minute. "To the left."

Because of those qualities the list of her dating some, one or two dates, goes on and on and on until it stopped, when she decided to fall in love. *"What's love got to do with it?"*

Alyson screamed through the voice mail, "Germaine pick up the telephone! Please." It was useless.

She redialed his number. He must wake up and answer. If he loved her he would hear her and respond. But instead she was forced to accept the fact. *Maybe he was not home. Maybe he's at the hospital."*

Finally he answered the telephone, sleepily. "Hello."

"Hey. I'm sorry to bother you. To call you so late but," She took a deep breath. He heard.

"What?" Dr. Ruiz was surprised and confused at the same time.

"Well." Alyson heard a small voice echoing in the back of her mind. *Don't trust him. He's apart of the plan. They wanted you to call him and then you will come and get you and take you to his house and they will kill you then and there. Kweisii is determine you will not live to see him suffer or pay for what he did. He would not give you the satisfaction. No one will ever suspect the good doctor. Remember Chip. You trusted Chip. But he was in the front seat of the Escalade when Kweisii kidnapped you. Remember Key's son, your favorite, Tommy you loved him as*

♥

much as your own son, he was driving the get away car.

"Never mind. I'm sorry to bother you."

"Don't hang up!" He pleaded "Alyson please talk to me. You have to learn to trust someone. I'm not the enemy. Everybody is not out to hurt you. Trust me please." He had become a psychiatrist promptly.

Alyson relaxed beyond her control. She may be overreacting. No way could the hotel and the Sheriff Department all be in cahoots with Kweisii, and Dr. Ruiz, what would he have to gain or lose?

How much power did she think Kweisii had?

She decided to check for the officer again. Maybe she had went to get a snack or to the restroom.

She held the telephone listening to Germaine repeating over and over again. "Alyson are you there?" He could hear her heavy breathing. She had not hung up. *Why won't she answer me?*

Finally she said, "Hold on Germaine." She peeped out the door once more. No one. Empty. "I'm sorry I just got a little nervous. I received some weird calls and the police officer guarding my door is nowhere to be found. She probably went for something to snack on. I'm overreacting. Sorry." She did not believe her own words.

"Maybe not. Pack your things! Stay put! I'll be right there. I'm on my way to get your. Stay put!"

"Okay." Alyson whispered with a sigh of relief.

Alyson was nervous. Germaine seemed too anxious for her to come to his house.

But she had no other choice. Her family was miles away. She did not know if she could trust the police force. They had abandoned her.

She thought about *Godfather III*. Where was her Michael? Why could he visit her at the hotel unexpectedly and sense that something was wrong and say to the receptionist "Do you know who my mother is? "Men are coming here to kill" her. People want her dead. We must move her to another room immediately." No such luck.

Her family was miles away believing she was safely being guarded by sworn in law officers, not the mob.

Kweisii seemed to be the mob and he had bad cops on his payroll.

Alyson conceded that she could stay in the hotel and worry all night long, if she made it through the night, or she could go to Germaine's house and wonder what the hell was going on, and wonder if she could make it through the night. Germaine's house seemed safer.

History tells us that Sam Davis, Jr. was the first black man to sleep at the white house while Nixon was president.

People teased about him sleeping with the one eye open and the other one in the glass of water was wide awake too. Alyson would sleep at Dr. Ruiz's house with both eyes open.

Paranoia set in. If she left with Germaine someone could possible see them together and follow them.

If she stayed at the hotel no one would see anything if they stuck in her room and killed her and slipped quiet away.

She was absorbed with fear with no relief in sight. Germaine's house was a better place. The maids were there, the chauffeur, surely someone would see something and justice would be served.

Dr. Germaine Ruiz arrived at the hotel approximately forty-minutes later. *He must have been speeding.*

He quickly hurried Alyson down the emergency exit and into his *Oh my God!* Black Escalade.

In the still of the nigh Alyson sat on the passenger side and starred at the back seat, sporadically. She could barely breathe.

Images of wanting to live flashed through her mind. With every turn so turned her whirling mind.

With every stoplight so stopped her heart. *Should I jump out and run? What's the use? I'm doomed.* Her heart beat faster and faster and pounded louder and louder.

The nigh was cool. Goose pumps protruded out of her epidermis. Sweat covered her forehead. Where would they dump her body?

Germaine broke the ice. "Are you okay? I know it's dark and scary at night but doing the day it's beautiful."

He was referring to the long dark road with only his headlights as their guide.

If a deer sprinted out it would be too late to stop even at forty miles per hour. The SUV would either swerve and flip over or the deer would be severely wounded or killed.

Ironically Alyson reminisced about her fist visit back to South Carolina after many years of living in Philly.

Her male cousin had taken her and Vern, her best friend and cousin, to the movies. On the way back he hit a fawn, not intentionally. But unfortunate things happen.

He got out the car and picked up Bambi and placed him in the truck. He said Mom-Pearl, their grandmother would be happy because they could have deer meat for days.

The entire thirty miles the fawn kicked at the roof of the trunk of the car and Alyson felt nauseated. Since then she would drive ten miles per hour in deer territory. That way she and the deer could survive if both got frozen in time.

"Please slow up. I don't want you to hit a deer." Without saying a word he slowed the car to a creepy twenty-five miles per hour.

They finally arrived at Dr. Ruiz's mansion, an old mansion with palm trees and grand entrance and balcony on top.

Alyson was escorted to a guess bedroom with antique rice post bed and antique drawers, plush carpet, a whiter billowed sitting unit located within a corner nook.

The room was cozy, invited, but dark. Alyson still in her pajamas the hotel feel on her knees, while Germaine watched, said her nightly prayers. "Lord, I come to you in the name of Jesus, I pray that your son and all his power surround me and project me from all my enemies. And I pray that the day come quickly when you make my enemies my footstool. I know no weapon form against me by those out to harm me will prosper. You are my guide and protector. Protect me as I journey through life and help me to be less conscious of my desires and more conscientious of others. In Jesus name I pray with thanksgiving. Always."

She had a reverie that Germaine's heart would melt, while listening to her prayer; consequently, he would let her live.

Wearily she climbed into bed and then Germaine tucked her in as if she was a two year old afraid of the boogeyman and her daddy had came in the middle of night to chase the nightmares away.

Alyson starred into those handsome dark brown eyes. The curls from his hair encircled his forehead. She had a strong urge to plea with him to let her live.

But instead she conceded this would be her last night in the land of the living. Then he was gone.

Alyson had made sure all her business was in order. A Living Will was created after her release from the hospital.

Since the kidnapping and rape she no longer took anything for granted.

Since finding out Key was a brother on the down low she no longer understood love.

Tazzy, Mitose and Da-Da would be better off financially with her dead than alive. That was a slight relief. That comforting thought forced her to sleep.

Alyson awoke the next morning with the sun blasting through the wide bay windows, trimmed in brown windowpane.

Where were the curtains or blinds? She was alive.

A few minutes later she heard a soft knock on the door and she quietly said, "Come in."

Germaine entered with a tray full of breakfast food. The bacon was sizzling; the toast was brown to perfection. The eggs easy side up and green tea. He was mocking her before killing her.

She smiled and sat up. She ate slowly. Enjoying her last meal. She whispered the prayer Jesus prayed in the Garden of Gethsemane, "Father if it be all possible, please take this cup from me. Nevertheless not my will be done but thy will."

Dr. Ruiz spoke, "You better get dressed. You have to be at the court house by 9:00 a.m.

This is torture. They're going to wait until the trial is over and then they'll kill me. Why then? Because Key has decided I needed to suffer. At least I have a few more weeks to live maybe between then I could come up with a strategy to live. She dressed very slowly. She had to treasure every moment of life.

Dr. Ruiz drove Alyson to the courthouse.

The courthouse was three block from the hospital. An old colonial style building, with white columns. The type of building Alyson, as a child in Sunday school, had imagined

♥

Samson pulling down the billows and killing all the Philistines. Would her life be destroyed because like Samson she told her secret of success to life to Key? She opened up her heart even though she had been burned many times before. Was Key her Delilah?

The court house was packed with reporters. Alyson felt uneasy and Germaine took noticed. "If the court dismisses before my shift ends at the hospital, call me and I'll send someone to get you. Do not walk the three blocks alone. Do you hear me?"

He really was behaving as if he cared. *He's good.*

"Okay." Alyson responded.

"Promise." He gripped her hand tight. "You'll be okay. You'll do fine." He walked her to the door of the courthouse. There she met the prosecutors and Germaine turned to walk down the marvel steps toward the hospital. She wanted to scream. *Don't leave me! I need you more than those sick patients.* But she kept quiet. Who could she trust? "See you later," was the only words she could mustard out.

The court proceedings were tedious and laborious. Experts were put on the stand to debate the DNA findings.

Alyson could not understand why they doubted Key had lied and said they had sex a day or two before the kidnapping.

But apparently some samples were collected from the rumble at the burnt shed and the prosecutor was trying to link them to Key and the defense team was hoping not to.

Alyson sat slightly behind her attorney's broad shoulders. The prosecutor was an African-American man, dark skinned, five foot ten inches tall and two hundred pounds. He was firm and did not take any shit. He was appreciative. He stood on his own merits with a broad smile and wide eyes. He didn't smile often. He was not attractive, but not unattractive.

That morning when Alyson informed him she was staying at a friend's house because she received weird calls at the hotel and how the officer disappeared on her. He telephoned the Richmond County Sheriff Department and caused quite a stir.

"What the fuck happened last night? My clients told me this morning she received strange calls last night and when she went to look for your officer she was no where to be found?"

"Hold on Attorney Jeter while I try and get to the bottom of this." Before the music took charge the Sheriff could be heard shouting, "Who the hell was on duty at the Lowes Hotel last night guarded the Santrock lady?

Attorney Jeter held for quit some while when he returned and said, "There's been a screw up on some paper work. No one was assigned to guard Mrs. Santrock."

Attorney Jeter interrupted. "Miss Santrock."

He continued. "Last night. But I can assure you this will not happen again. She will be guarded tonight and well protected."

If you planning on guarding her you would have to guard her at Dr. Germaine Ruiz's home. He seem to be doing a better job protecting her than your sorry for an excuse department." He flipped his cell phone down.

"Miss Santrock."

"Call me Alyson. My name is Alyson."

He smiled, "If you like, I can come by Dr. Ruiz's house tonight and help him guard you." He said shyly. "But only if you want me too and it'll make you feel safer. We're dealing with some powerful people."

"No. I'll be fine." Dealing with one man with a crush was more than enough for her to swallow. She was already beginning to choke.

Sitting in the courtroom being in Key's presence was not a comfortable emotionally and Key added to the direst.

Every time Alyson leaned upward she caught his eye. He was

scowling her for justifiable reasons. He was on his way to jail and hell in a hand basket.

Saul sat directly behind him. Not unusual. The thought of the two of them together pulsated her mind.

She felt a migraine coming, creeping up like a fox about to attack a rabbit.

The secret was out. Key had found a love that would endure the test of time. She had yet to discover that love. She envied Saul and Key, nauseatingly.

The judged recessed the court proceedings around 1:00 p.m. Court to convene at 10:00 a.m. the next morning. After a forensic investigator testified the entire morning, laboriously.

Standing in the almost empty courtroom Alyson telephone Dr.

Germaine Ruiz. He could not be summoned. He was in surgery. He was do out of surgery around 3:00 p.m. She decided two hours of shopping was good for the soul.

Prior to, she went into the bathroom and disguised herself. The huge eye glasses and wide hat, the change of jackets and from heels to flats made shopping safe. Shopping was a relief.

It made her believe life was back to "normal." No one recognized her. Everybody was just going along minding their own business, without a clue that she was in Virginia not by choice but force because her gay ex-boyfriend tried to kill her.

Exhausted from shopping. Alyson walked the five blocks from the mall to the hospital. When Germaine existed the hospital door heading toward the courtroom to pick her up he was surprised to find her setting on the bench outside the hospital feeding the bread left over from her hot dog to birds. It was like being in Venice, at the St. Mark's Square.

"I heard if you feed them more would come. Is that your plan?"

He said the word plan. What was his plan?

"No I don't have a plan. I take one day at a time."

"I see. So you're living off compulsion instead of rationality. Because the fact that you are here instead of the courtroom let's me know that you take one day at a time because you have decided that each day maybe your last. Seem depression. Just living for the moment."

She wanted to be realistic. "Each day maybe my last." As if he didn't know.

"So, you're telling me." He sat down next to her. He smelled freshly showered. Safeguard soap. Must have been a messy operation. "That you have no plans for the future. That your future is so bleak that it's not worth trying to prepare for."

"I have prepared for the future. I have a Living Will."

He laughed. "That's your idea of preparing for the future. How about marriage, more children, write more books, or/and travel around the world."

"I don't think about those things anymore. Anyway I cannot have anymore children. My ob/gyn doctor said he don't understand how this body ever carried children."

"But it did. Miracles do happen."

"To other people." She had lost her faith.

"Not just to other people to you too. You're here right now alive and healthy. I just finish operating on a young man who had a motorcycle accident. The paramedics radioed in and said he would be dead on arrival. But when he arrived with his praying mother holding his hand, I felt a slight pulse. I started the operating procedures to stop the internal bleeding and his mother made her contact with God. He is in Intensive Care right now with warm blood running through his veins, and a steady heart rate. Is not warm blood running through your veins?"

"If my blood is warmed then my mind is playing tricks on me because

♥

the signals I received from it is telling me its numb but most likely cold."

"Alyson I should not have to tell you this but sometimes we have to control our thoughts not let them control us. You need to shake off this depression and start living again. Enough of me fussing, are you hungry?"

"No I just ate a hot dog."

"When did you start back eating hot dogs?"

"When I started living one day at a time."

After her kidnapping, physical assault and rape, while being discharged from the hospital, Dr. Ruiz had ordered her to stay away from hot dogs, bologna, and red meat.

"How about dessert. The Oliver Garden is around the corner."

"Dessert it is."

♥♥♥♥♥

Did Kweisii "Key"

Mfumey have powerful friends in Virginia? This was the pressing unanswered question.

The Virginia trial came in the middle of the senate race in Maryland. Some say the trial was helping Mfumey win the senate seat and some claimed it was hurting him.

The white conservative stated it was helping him because blacks stick together when one commits immoral acts.

They used the fact that blacks stuck by President Bill Clinton with his infidelity. Blacks stuck by the Reverend Jessie Jackson, Sr. with his infidelity. They idolized Dr. Martin Luther King, Jr. in spite of his infidelity.

They were predicting that the blacks would come out in record numbers and support Mfumey during the primary election.

They proclaimed that the Democrats were making a mistake shunning Mfumey for the white man and they would pay during the primary election big time.

The African-American Democrats seemed to be saying. "Conservatives just want us to vote for Mfumey because their man have a better chance of winning against Mfumey than Cardine.

Conservatives don't tell us who to vote for. We can see through their games. We cannot be tricked. Those days are over when the master persuaded us to tell where a run away slave was hiding promising no recourse and then beating him or her to death. We can see through the scheme. We see the bigger picture. Although Mfumey is black we just don't vote for a person because he's black. We can assess the issues. If Mfumey has lied and deceived all these years why would we trust him to represent us in the senate? Don't play us for a fool. We won't vote for Mfumey." Maybe Alyson could get a fair trial.

Three weeks into the trial while the jury deliberated, the exact date of the Democratic Primary Election, Alyson was trying to sleep at Dr. Germaine Ruiz's comfortable home.

It was a rainy night, stormy, and dark, a mackerel sky, with specks of stars only visible with lightning.

Alyson wanted to crawl under the quilt and smother herself in sleep in hopes of sleeping the night away. Virginia was feeling the affects of Tropical Storm Isabella. She had ribbed apart Florida. She had annihilated the coast of South Carolina, Myrtle Beach, hit the hardest. Ten million dollars worth of damage. It would takes months to rebuild.

Myrtle Beach, picturesque, peaceful, along the Carolina's coast, silent in ignorance, but welcoming to visitors, a safe haven for the hid away racist, a frequent vacation of Alyson, not Kweisii, he was boycotting Myrtle Beach. They were a happy couple then. She was blest and he was successful. The truth was hidden safely away under the weight of the Atlantic Ocean.

Alyson laid in Dr. Ruiz's, "Germany" house. She had

nicknamed him Germany. She had nicknamed Kweisii Key because she believed he would forever hold the key to her heart.

Germany had become her German Shepherd, her guardian angel, and her best friend. During her college days she had a dog named Angel, a white, green eyed albino, full-breed German Shepherd, female. She had rescued her from an abusive home, when the dog was only one year old.

At first the dog was timid and would shake with fear at the sight of a male figure.

She was extremely difficult to housebreak. But normal behavior was evident. She would get in the trash can if Alyson left the lid off. She would chew up a new pair of shoes of hers, the most difficult act to accept.

She immediately jumped on Alyson's forbidden bed the moment Alyson left the house. She left strands of DNA all over the bed.

Disciplining her was something Alyson avoided. Love was more warranted. Convincing Angel of her love and then slowly implementing discipline was Alyson's motto. The convincing of love lasting almost a year. Then enough was enough.

Angel was taking advantage of the situation. Rules were enforced. "Do not get up on the furniture. No matter how I bath you, I still smell dog. You are a little too big for newspaper. The backyard is this way." Now the trash it was Alyson's fault. She had to remember to keep the lid on, in addition, her closet door closed, tightly.

As a result of disciplining Angel, the dog life of Angel and Alyson prove to be loveable, cuddling and durable.

However, Angel's feelings toward male humans, a male had abused her too, did not change.

When Alyson male friend came to pick her up on dates, he was not allowed to make one move in her house. He had to sit on the couch pensively until Alyson was dressed and ready. Alyson's male friend could not turn on the television on. If he made a move toward any object in the house, Angel would growl at him. He could not reach for the radio unless Angel barked at him.

Chris, short brown, sneaky eyes, unfaithful, said teasingly, "Your dog's a lesbian." Alyson laughed.

Chip told her once women become lesbians because they are hurt so many times by men. But if we could only learned from the lower primates. Angel was no lesbian. When Alyson decided to breed her with another German Shepherd she had no problem yielding to the temptation.

Germaine had in a sense became Alyson and Alyson was Angel. He was degage to love her unconditionally, wounded and abused, as she did Angel.

She was brought into his home and cared for with patience and understanding.

He gave her the opportunity to grow, adapt, and adjust to life once again. He was her protector.

He sat between her and Kweisii mentally and physically, preventing

Kweisii from touching any aspect of her life, from ever again wounding her.

She often wondered if nicknaming Germaine Germany, expecting him to continue to protect her, would backfire on her, as Key who held the key to her heart, unlocked it and ripped it apart.

Alyson lay in bed at peace. Enraptured in the sector of the world when others believe there was peace before a storm but the winds and the waves knew better. They beat fiercely and bombarding against each other.

Alyson lay reflecting on the trial. Kweisii's attorney were putting up a great argument.

She was a woman scorn who was angry that Kweisii no longer wanted to date her. So she did write *N.A.C.P.*

II National Association of the Collard Pew to destroy him and his career.

She was successful. He was losing the senate seat, according to Baltimore news reports. A position he had lived the past twenty-five years of his life planning for.

His attorney's words echoed in her mind, "She is so revengeful and obsessive, she would even blame him for kidnapping and raping her, which is obscured. She would do anything to destroy him permanently."

They argued Alyson's book did not have the affect on Kweisii's career as she hoped so she seized the opportunity to blame Kweisii for something he had nothing do with.

The prosecutor found many loop holes in the defense team's argument, but would the jurors?

Alyson had no known enemies other than Mfumey. She had not dated since the revelation of his homosexuality. She had trouble trusting. She basically led an introverted lifestyle, contracting sporadically with various school systems for work but no social life, Kweisii had demolished that.

Although the defense searched for possible enemies they could not produce any witness to testify that Alyson was not liked or had caused or attacked another man other than Kweisii.

The prosecutor put several of Alyson's past male friends on the stand and although most had their own set of fame, high school basketball star, college basketball star, professional basketball and football players, none testified during or agreed during cross examination that Alyson had tried to destroy them in any way form or fashion. At least one sexual preference had been questioned for years and Alyson had respectfully withheld the truth.

It's a given, a fifty year old man, never been married, babies by several women, down low.

Alyson had been the idea girlfriend and they the creeps, regretting for the rest of their lives that they let her slip through their fingers. Alyson on the other hand had walked away from the relationships holding tight to her dignity with all her might. She had lost with Kweisii. She loved him too hard.

The prosecutor argued during his closing arguments, "walking away peaceful without the need for a tell all book was impossible because unlike

Kweisii these men really loved Alyson, the relationship was genuine and healthy, and the break-ups were under 'normal' circumstances.

No history of physical or emotional abuse by any of the other men. In contrast, the relationship with Kweisii Mfumey was unusual and deceptive."

Alyson appeared as a deflowered female. Would the twelve jurors, eight men; four African-American men, two Latino men and two Caucasians, — four females two black female one Latino, one Asian, find Key guilty? What experiences did these individuals have that would break or make the case?

Alyson knew the truth. She had indeed written the book because she was scorn. She was angry and she believed it was not fair for Kweisii to be at peace in his deceptive world and she at war in her scornful state. But she also knew if she did not expose him he would strike again and she as a religious born again believer in Christ, had to trust all this happened for a reason. And she had to turn the evil into good. She had to help women who have or will deal with men of Kweisii's caliber. She believed in preventive measures. She had to turn evil into good. She had to help women who have or will or to prevent this from happening to anyone else. This was her civil duty.

In that aspect she was correct, she had succeeded. She had hoped Kweisii would go away but he surged with vengeance However, he had settled in with Saul Carll.

His disregard and adventitious attitude toward woman would no longer spread abroad. The truth about his sexual preference had set some women free. It had spread like wildflower.

This was her main goal. For women to become more aware of the symptoms of brothers on the down low. Alyson knew America has forgiven President Bill Clinton for adultery, and Reverend Jessie Jackson, Sr., as well, so they were more likely to forgive Kweisii for his deception.

America was a sexiest country. The men ruled. Not the majority, but a lot of women remained gullible and acceptance and persuaded by whatever a man told them.

Women were taught to "player hate" on each other, this way if a man was caught cheating, it was the woman's fought. Men are weak. Women are strong. The Bible speaks of quite the contrary. Women are the weaker vessel. If he cheat it was because the temptress woman tempted him. Bullshit!

If a man cheat, it is because he is "drawn away by his own lust."

The story in the Bible, about the woman being caught in adulterous was popular during President Bill Clinton and Revered Jesse Jackson's debacle. The law said, back in the New Testament times, that when a couple was caught in adultery the woman was stoned to death.

But hold up, wait a minute, what did the law say about the man? When President Bill Clinton was caught in adultery many religious people supported him by saying "He that be without sin cast ye the first stone." Yes these are the words of Jesus. But the words should have applied to

Monica Lewinsky, as well as President Bill Clinton who would have been spared anyway. Monica was the weaker vessel. Alyson was aware that the culture she lived in, sensitivity seemed to go to the deceiver and somehow the victim is to blame for not knowing better or being wiser.

Forgiveness was always at Kweisii's door. So why did he play the game in the first place?

Were the jurors Republican or Democrats? How many of the jurors sympathized with Rev. Jackson and President Clinton? Did jurors in Richmond have family members in Maryland who voted for Key to become Maryland next United States Senate? Would Mfumey be set free?

Mfumey sat through the court proceedings descending.

Alyson sat up in bed. She reached over and flipped on the lamp's light switch. She gripped the remote control.

The jurors were sequestered and the deliberation had extended another day. The fourth day of deliberation. *What was taken them so long? What specific detailed were they baffled about?*

She flipped on the eleven o'clock news. Reporter Janey Millery was reporting "Where is Mfumey? We have been looking for Mfumey since eight o'clock a.m. We have text messaged his campaign manager and we have contacted his campaign headquarters. It is eleven eighteen and no one has heard from Mfumey." She displayed a schedule Kweisii was suppose to follow for the day. He was suppose to be at Ray Lewis' restaurant in Saint Michaels at 12:19 p.m. but he did show up.

She questioned a voter, "Have you seen Mr. Mfumey?"

"No and I don't care."

She was a middle age black woman. Janey Millery turned to an elderly black male.

"Have you seen Mfumey?"

He responded, "No and maybe he has went somewhere and sat down."

Next she turned to a crowd of black voters. "Have any of you seen Mr. Mfumey?"

They all shouted in unison, "No!"

"I'm Janey Millery reporting live from Baltimore County. Back to you at WBAL news."

She stressed the word news.

Alyson became a freight. Where was Mfumey?

Two days prior she had read in the Baltimore newspaper about the debate between him and Cardine. Cardine had finally addressed Kweisii dishonesty and secrets.

Cardine responded to Kweisii accusations that he was dishonest and said he takes on the drug companies when actually he was in the drug company's pocket. "You say that I am dishonest. I have been a congressman for thirty years and married over forty years. My contingents know where I stand in all areas. I have taken on the drug companies. I am a heterosexual and I have nothing to hide." The room went silent.

Kweisii glared at Saul across the podium in the back and never responded to the real deal. He did what he does best, defocused.

Kweisii, "I am a fighter. If you put me in office I promise I will fight for equal education."

Mr. Mfumey, during his run for the senate seat strongly supported gay marriages. He said he believed marriage was what God said in the Bible earlier in his life but circumstances has forced him to see things different than what the word of God states. This was the first time he had whispered an honest statement.

Subsequently, black ministers within the city of Baltimore supported him and his run for United States senate. It would be wise for their church members to take a close or closer look at those minister's lifestyle. Some are in the closet. Don't be afraid to open the closet of some men of God they need exposure too. Perpetrating a fraud.

Consequently some Baltimoreans present at the black community church during the debate were furious and disappointed. He was their black hope. Yet they had just discovered the game he had been playing for years.

The majority of the elderly people were angry because they were disgusted with his sexual preference.

The younger generation were angry that he did not have the courage to be what he was a homosexual.

The middle-age females were despondent. Their fantasies of one day becoming his wife crumbled. Their conquest was shattered. The middle age heterosexual men were disappointed, another black male making them appear all bad.

The gay men were hopeful. Maybe he was not faithful to Saul and they could one day have an affair with him.

The lesbians were content they knew all alone. They had been proven correct.

Kweisii game board grumbled. Had he lost the game?

The juror's decision would answer that question. Would they placate his involvement in the crime?

The jurors were sequestered to avoid gaining access to this information.

During the trial the prosecutors and defense team shied away from his homosexuality.

The judge had decided his sexual preference was irrelevant to the case. It was his personal business.

Forget the fact that his sexual preference was the reason *N.A.C.P. Notations Admix the Collard Pew* and

N.A.C.P. II National Association of the Collard Pew were written. If he was going around deceiving people what else was he capable of?

Something was strange about courts deciding in favor of deceptive men. Why did Terri McMillan have to give Jonathan Plummer alimony money after he used and lied and deceived her for so many years? A discussion concerning Terri McMillan and Jonathan Plummer was being heard over the radio. The host asked another radio host, "When do you think she found out?" The response was "She should have known the day she met him." Then laughter.

Yes, Alyson agreed, she should have known. His gay radar glowed fluorescent. Kweisii's gay radar was opaque.

The jurors were forbidden to read Alyson's books and any potential juror who had read one or all were dismissed from jury duty.

Several potential jurors were dismissed for reading *Nearsighted Child*, a novel by Alyson about surviving incest and being poor. Nothing about Kweisii.

But the judge thought those who read her books would be swayed by any persuasive statements. Persuasive statements are for closing arguments in a trial.

Writers tell non-fiction and fiction stories. Alyson believed the jurors should have access to the "whole truth and nothing but the truth." She did not understand the legal system in America.

Enough thoughts about Kweisii, the jurors, and the trial. Alyson

♥

flipped off the television. She clicked off the lamp. She listened to the monotonous ticking away of her bedroom clock. The huge grandfather clock standing upright and proud in its position chimed midnight.

She wondered if Germaine was fast asleep. Could he sleep through the wind and tree limbs swiping the windows with eerie shapes and scary sounds. She surely could not. If she went to his bedroom she would probably be asking for something she was not ready to receive.

Germaine was understanding but he was a man. She still hoped. Doubts still lingered. *Was he a pond sent by Mfumey to take her body to a surgical suite and dissect it piece by piece, beyond anyone's possibility of identification? Was he poisoning her slowing with an undetected pesticide?*

Would he dissect her body and donate the parts to science or donate her body as a codifier to University of Virginia Medical School as a Jane Doe and her disappearance being explained away as she was too ashamed of her actions and fled to Europe?

Her heart pounded inside her chest. Her anxiety level rose. Sleep escaped her. She had conceded that her wild thoughts would control her for the remaining of the night. "Weeping my endure for a night but joy come in the morning." Oh how she longed for joy of the morning.

Alyson heard an unusual noise inside the house. Germaine's house was extremely quiet at night. So any noise would penetrate. Maybe it was the maid or Germaine going down for a late night snack. She decided if it

♥

was Germaine she would go down stairs and talk with him, this should help the joy in the morning come faster.

She stepped into the hallway. It was pitched dark. A shadow of Germaine appeared. "Is everything okay?" She asked.

"I don't know. I guess the storm knocked out the lights."

He headed down the stairs leaving her standing in the hallway deserted and lonely like a kitten wondering through an alley missing the meows of her mother.

Slowly she took one step at a time. She finally reached the bottom step. Standing in the dark of the silence of the storm she whispered, "Germaine. Germaine." She quivered and whispered "Germaine" again. She wondered why she was whispering.

There was no one else to wake up. She felt an old breeze.

Walking in the alcove she studied the room owlishly. Curtains were swaying and a window was broken. "Oh my God!" She turned to run away but someone grabbed her and held her mouth shut and a gun to her head. "Shut-Up! If you move or scream, I'll kill you for sure this time." Kweisii's became catapulted and his voice was peeved. He slowly removed his hand from her mouth. "Just listen."

She nodded with a glare. He grabbed her neck tight. She could barely breathe. "You think you are so smart. You bitch. What makes you think you can go around destroying my career? Everything was perfectly planned, until you wrote your shitty books. Now I'll lose the senate race. Why? Because you decided to tell people I could not be trusted. You caused me my job at the N.A.C.P. and now the U.S. senate. The jurors will probably find me guilty and sentenced me to life in prison so what do I have to lose? You whore."

Alyson stood with her hands trembling and her body shaking in shock. He turned her to face him. "Look at me! Look at me and see what you turned me into! A monster!" His skin was dark, teeth yellowish. He smelled of old clothes and alcohol. He had a myriad of questions. "Is this what you wanted? You like destroying people? Are you that hateful? Didn't you know we could have had it all? Don't you know many women would have been willing to play the game? Okay, you got it your way, but now it'll be my way." She stared beyond her moans.

The curtains flew up with the wind and Germany stood behind them. He had an object in his hand. Easing up slithering, he crushed Mfumey over the head. Kweisii fell to the floor. He gripped Germany by the angles and pulled him face down to the floor. Alyson screamed and ran behind the couch.

A few minutes later she heard police sirens then a single gunshot. Both men laid silent. Her sobs were audibly.

She slowly crawled on her hands and knees, with a moistened face toward the motionless bodies. If Germaine was dead she was willing to die too.

In a split second one man threw the other man's limb body over onto the floor.

Faced up, the former city councilman, the former congressman, the former president and chief executive officer of the N.A.C.P., the former candidate for the United States senate, Kweisii Mfumey, was lying on the cold packed floor motionless with a pool of blood flowing from his nose, ears and mouth. A gasped with pupils fixed. He was dead.

Alyson pulled at Germany. Was he hurt too? He fell back with his hands behind his head breathing heavy. She kissed him over and over again.

"Are you all right?" He whispered.

"Yes." She was never so safe.

He lifted himself up and then Alyson. She sat on his lap. "Duck!" He shouted. She quickly responded.

A bullet just missed her head and shattered a vase. Then a stern voice said "Drop it!" The gunman dropped his weapon immediately without resistance.

The officer read the gunman his rights. "Saul Carll Swanne you have the right to remain silent anything you say can and will be held against you in the court of law."

Saul Carll Swanne was sentenced to fifteen years in prison without parole.

♥♥♥♥♥

Exactly One Year Later

Teaching science to a classroom full of middle high school eight graders,

Alyson was semi content. A discussion lead to the physical structure of the human brain and then took a discussion on the dynamics of the brain.

She educated her students to the fact that we as humans only use about ten percent of our brain. The other ninety percent was vibrated in the atmosphere of life.

"Our reasoning is controlled by the frontal lobe. The frontal lobes takes a turn during adolescence. Do you know that a nine year old can reason better than you all can right now."

Collectively, "No way!"

"It's true.   Adolescents lack reasoning and need a lot of guidance. That's why some of you come in here and in spite of the rules being written and reinforced everyday you still violate them. Lack of reasoning."

"That's John!" One of the students shouted out.

The classroom laughs. Laughter was okay.

"As a result of this discussion our motto for this class the remaining of the school term is I have a brain and I will use it."

What   prompted   Alyson's discussion on the brain was two boys who came into the class jumping over chairs, wrestling and throwing small objects. She sat watching them for a few minutes, ten minutes to be exact.

She was curious how long it would take for them to settle down. It darned on her that they were not taking the initiative on their own to do what was right so verbal prompting by way of raising her voice was necessary. "Sit down and get quiet and start your warm-up!"

You would think after five months of school and carrying out the same routine everyday they would have got it. They ignored her verbal demand.

This was not unusual for these two boys and safe to say unfortunate for their lives. They were on a down ward spiral. Spinning fast.

Once Alyson got the boys to settle down and be quiet she began her lecture on the brain. Her therapy self was returning.

She had thought teaching could suppress it. Her complete healing was nigh. She had a desire to help others.

She imagined these boys being like Key one day. He talked about how he misbehaved in school and no doubt they were struggling with some internal and external issues but, unlike Key, who apparently gave his brain to a tiger, an animal who wants to devour, or maybe an ape who's capable of manipulated and deceiving, or maybe a muskrat who lack the sense of love and dedication, these boys had to come clean and be honest with themselves or maybe one day they would sink into the quicksand that they themselves were stirring.

Addressing the boys, Alyson said. "I'm sad to say that John and

Sean don't have a brain." Everyone in the room became quiet. She continued loudly, "Because if they had a brain surely it would have registered to them by now the procedure to following when entering the class. School started five months ago. If they had a brain they would have learned the daily routine. Our brain automatically registered what is expected in given situation. Surely if they had a brain it would have instinctually played the script of behavior expectations in their science class.

But since they don't have a brain they don't know how to behave from day-to-day. I had better success at teaching a male tree kangaroo, marsupial, to not kill his baby, joey within sixty days than I've had teaching you boys what to do when you come into my classroom."

From that day forward Alyson had the students and parents sign a contract stating they understood how students are expected to behave in class which included the motto "I have a brain and I promise to use it."

It was comical for Alyson to walk through the hallways of the school and hear one student say to another, "You have a brain, use it." Or "You're not using your brain." Or "Try and use more than ten percent of your brain." Or "Where's your brain? Did you try and give your brain to the tree kangaroo and he threw it back." That one was Alyson's favorite.

The students agreed to use their brains and the parents agreed to encourage the students to use their brains.

The challenge was set forth. If a student used his or her brain at the end of class they received a brain sticker. If a student collected fifty brain stickers they could use their brain by touring Washington, D.C. in the month of May.

If a student did not use his or her brain during class they would have to explain via homework assignment why they failed to use his or her brain and what animal they would try and convince to take his or her brain and explain why the lower primate would probably rejected the brain.

If the animals accepted the brain then the argument must be made, why did he or she think their brain suited better in the lower primates' head than his or hers? What behaviors the lower primate demonstrated that are similar to the student's behavior? The students had a choice between a rodent, deer, donkey, horse, snake, alligator, crocodile, giraffe, elephant, lion, tiger, and any animal they could think of.

They summed up the homework by explaining why they needed their brain back and what they would do to keep it. An enjoyable moment in Alyson's life time.

Later that afternoon, Alyson would find herself sitting in a volleyball game at Boe High School. Tazzy had forsaken her many years of tap, ballet, and jazz dance classes for the sport of volleyball. Following in her mother's footstep, a three time most valuable player, Tazzy embraced the sport of volleyball.

Sports are good for children. Statistic supports that children who play sports are more likely to stay in school and pass all their course work. Tazzy an all out honors student was validating those statistics.

Alyson supported parenthood to the fullest. She believed that loving and caring and being their for her children was one task she could not fail to fulfill.

She attended all Tazzy extra-curricular activities as she did Mitose, from escorting her dance competition team to Orlando, Florida to perform at the Disney Parade or to the Orange Bowl in Miami Florida half-time performance.

Tazzy was fulfilling dreams Alyson had long abandoned. Tazzy's life had more to offer than rejection and pain.

One particular volleyball game in walks a tall dark handsome man, in the true since, six foot two, dark skinned, bright teeth, and inquiring bright beautiful sexy eyes. He caught Alyson's eye, a difficult thing to do.

Alyson ten pounds more, with a head full of hair. During her debacle with Mfumey she had lost weight, went back to her high school size three, and as the norm when she was stressed she cut her hair extremely short all over, typical of a stressed woman, and her demeanor was a constant languid.

Her smile had returned thanks to several of Tazzy's friends. They at that present moment added life to her lifeless ness.

Monica, overweight, tall brown, quiet and shy full of natural pretty, Alyson wondered what man would break her heart and turn her into a boisterous mean woman. Janae, short, "a brick house," long black hair, beautiful, was vibrations and lively. Alyson wondered what man would quince her spirit and make her a shy intimidating woman. Christa, bold, coca brown skin, tall, and talented, a bit aggressive, demanding, having the drive to fight for what she wanted. What man would make her second guess herself?

But at that moment, at that volleyball game, Alyson watched the girls on the floor of the court and realized they offered to her what she had lost.

Alyson also played volleyball. She was also outspoken, boisterous, and self-confident at one time or another.

Then there was Tazzy, smart, bright, confident, cute, and shy. Shier than Alyson and Mitose, but both

Alyson's children were more friendlier than she; more accepting of people and trusting than Alyson ever was or ever will be.

Some scars don't dissipate. What man would attempt to weaken Tazzy's strengths and destroy her willfulness? None if Alyson could had a say or could help

All the girls had little boyfriends, who would eventually play on the basketball team. Tazzy friend Derek was six foot three inches tall, dark with thick eyebrows, handsome. Monica's friend David was six foot two inches tall, brown with small questionable eyes.

Christa friend Dandre short and stocky, all offered to the girls a hope beyond the starry skies that the one love they had wish for had found them.

Janae's friend was of unique interest to Alyson, because it was her friend whose dad walked into the gym and caught Alyson's wounded spirit.

The sight of him momentary ceased the constant spend of the whirlwind in Alyson's mind.

It was he who appeared to be caressing her spastic heart. It was he, Terrace Lurkins from Midton.

Alyson could not remember the last time she had felt such strong emotions for a man.

Upon impulse the moment returned like a momma bird to her nest. It was eerily similar to the day in the restaurant when Kweisii motioned her. Alyson recalled.

It was a bright sunny perfect irresistible summer May day in Washington, District of Columbia, spring had dripped away. The flowers were glowing. The sky was bright and blue. Everyone seated on the green lawn of the football field at Howard University had slowed down to watch the warming sunshine springing over the graduates. It took us several hours to find parking. Howard University graduation had brought people from all over the globe.

My niece, Dawn Deed was fulfilling a dream and a goal she had set back in elementary school. She had promised her mother that she would graduate from Howard University. The Lord had made a way, financially, emotionally, and cognitively and that goal was accomplished. At least one of her dreams had come true. She had accomplished this goal and accomplished it with honors, graduating magnum cum laude. I was proud of her and I would not have missed the opportunity to witness her graduation from Howard University for anything. She was the first one in our family to graduate from a Historical Black College.

I wanted to seize the opportunity to get a glimpse of those beaming graduates' faces apparently forced, to tackle the world. These granted me the opportunity to reminiscence and reflect on my graduation ceremonies, my undergraduate graduation ceremony from Temple University holding it fondest memory. I reflected on the popping of the champagne bottles' corks and the balloons being bounced from one graduate to another, and President Lacrosse declaring that although we had turned our graduation ceremony into a party, we did not party as hard as the graduating class before us—what a joy. We all laughed. That was not our goal. We just wanted to celebrate. We deserved it. The long hours of studying and hanging in there when friends were being "kicked out" by the masses for not maintaining the required grade point average, paid off for us. We were under a lot of pressure and the pressure had been released.

I was indeed familiar with the glow on Dawn's face. I was proud, the proud aunt, and I wished her the best of luck with her career goals and in life. She had planned to return to Howard University for her

Master's Degree in Education then she would pursue a law degree at Temple University.

Dawn wanted to show off the sites of Washington, D.C. Washington, D.C. had been her home for the past four years. Dawn took pride in knowing the names of buildings and sites located in Historical Washington, D.C. Unlike most of us she immediately recognized more sites than the Pentagon and the White House. She knew the names of Lincoln Memorial, Jefferson Memorial, the United States Capital Building, the United States Supreme Court Building and the Library of Congress.

For lunch Dawn escorted us, proudly without removing her blue graduation gown and golden tassel, to a restaurant named Geofrey. The seafood restaurant was located along the Potomac River, an all you can eat place, buffet style, restaurant. She recognized there were individuals in her family which one portion of a meal was not enough.

Dawn's eyes as crystal-clear as they always were lined up with the blue sky and the brightly dazed reflected like the sun off a crystal glass. Dawn, fair skinned and tall five foot nine inches tall. Although my sister, average five foot four inches her husband was short five foot six inches tall. Their three children took after my father's family. Our father, six foot three inches tall and slim fair skinned with dark curly hair and charcoal brown eyes, thin faced and huge lips were *often mistaken for Latino. Dawn had a lot going for her other than a beautiful face and it did not take me long to notice the gifts God had placed within her.*

During the summer months I would baby-sit my nieces and nephews for spending money. Dawn and Dana were two nieces born around the same time. I had the privilege of babysitting the two of them during the summer months. Dana was feisty and challenging. Dawn was calm and obedient.

Although fourteen years old I recognized I could make my babysitting job easy or hard. I decided to make it easy. I had a schedule. In the mornings I would minister "education time:" reading, coloring and drawing, and Sesame Place lessons. At noon I fed them lunch and then one P.M. was naptime. I would lay Dawn and Dana in the bed, and then I would say my afternoon prayers. Then I would comfortably watch, on my small thirteen-inch black and white television set, Gilligan's Island and Good Times, my favorite television sitcoms, while Dana and Dawn fell peacefully asleep. Before falling asleep, Dawn would crawl out of bed and kneel beside me and at the tender age of one her prayers consisted of calling on the name of Jesus over and over again. Dana would stare at us bleakly but she never joined us in prayer. The outcome of Dawn's life in comparisons to Dana was a result of the quest for what was right.

Geofrey's was a nice seafood restaurant enclosed by the

surrounding Potomac River and sliding patio doors and distinctive bay windows rendering a peaceful view of the Potomac River. To no surprise the restaurant was crowded. Other graduates had the same idea and wanted to display the seafood restaurant to their families. We had a long wait.

I stood in the lobby talking with my family and my cousin, Carle. She had assisted in helping me drive from Columbia. Carle and I glowed as we talked about the happy day and laughed at all the problems we encountered which delayed our trip to Washington, D.C. from Columbia. Everything hindered us from leaving Columbia on time. I could not find my son, who had gone to the store with his friends and took forever to come back.   Finally, I left him in Columbia.   The traffic in Virginia was horrendous.   But we made it and made it in enough time to get some rest and wake up bright and early and attend the graduation. I dressed in a teal blue ankle length silk skirt by Diane Von and Tommy Hilfiger navy blue blouse and a pair of blue sandals by DKNY, a pocketbook by Louie Vuitton. Carle dressed in a Gloria Vanderbilt black nylon dress with black pumps accessorized by Aigner bag. Carle was twelve years older than me, but the years had narrowed. I often said I caught up with her. Carle, short, plump and brown, commercial eyes and a toothless grin, which she often displayed without embarrassment, was my riding partner.

♥

A man stared in my mouth while I communicated with my family. He was there, in the lobby, with a woman and I looked to her to rescue me from her hound. But she did not in particular mind that he had taken a liking to me. He was a very attractive man but I was not there to pick up a man, but to celebrate my niece's graduation. I made every attempt to ignore him.

After being seated the waitress, Caucasian, short and stocky, light brown shoulder length hair, white shirt and black pants with a tablecloth wrapped around her waist as an apron, distributed our party's silverware and plates. We all charged to the buffet tables. When I arrived at the seafood bar the man from the lobby had followed me, and flirtatiously picked up every item I chose on the menu. I was taking aback. I chose for an appetizer, Seared Ahi tuna, he chose the same. I chose for a meal Sonoma green salad, fried calamari and cheese bread. He chose the same with additions, hot and country shrimp, trout, oysters, and chilled Alaskan king crab. Try eating like me and you'll be anorexia thin. He had figured that out.

Back in my seat I realized he had sat diagonally in front of me and his female friend sat to his left. I looked from her to him then from him to her. He shook his head. Oh she's a relative. I understood why he was disregarding her. A few minutes later he walked past our table and grabbed the back of my chair, pulling on my bra strap. He was bold but in a way I liked it very much. He stood in a small hallway adjacent from my seat waiting for the elevator with a young man. Before walking on the elevator he motioned for me to follow him. I hesitated.

A few minutes later I exited by way of the stairs. I stood in the lobby pretending I was waiting for my other party to join me.

Security approached, short five foot three inches tall, with green eyes and reddish taped hair, wearing a pair of black pants and white shirt, and he spoke, "Hey what's your name? Mr. Mfumey wants to take a picture with you." I had not noticed the security man prior. It was eerie that he was so near but so far. How freaky.

"With me?" I answered with a trembling voice. I was surprised and a little nervous.

"Yeah." He flashed a friendly smile.

"Where is he?" My eyes searched the lobby.

"Behind there." He pointed to a corridor by the exit door. The corridor hosted the pay telephone booths and the doors to the public laboratories. The man from the lobby leaned against a pay telephone booth pretending to be talking on the telephone.

"Should I go?" Looking at Carle. She had joined me in the lobby before the rest of the family. I was skeptical.

"Go ahead. What do you have to lose?" Carle replied thoughtfully.

"Okay. Lead the way."

I stood before the man from the lobby my hands sweaty and heart pounded.

"Hi! What's your name?" Mr. Mfumey inquired.

"Alyson." I was uneasy.

"Where are you from?" He tried to calm my nerves.

"Columbia."

"Okay, okay you're gorgeous." He said with an evasive smile.

"Thanks."

We posed for the picture he rubbed up and down my back and even brushed against my buttocks. He was a flirt.

He looked momentarily sheepish. "I'll like to get to know you..."

"Really, really me?" I was puzzled.

"Really." He was laughing.

"Me?" I relented.

"Why not?" He stared meaningfully.

"I don't know." I was uncomfortable but he was interested

He wrote down my number on the program from the graduation. He did not give me his and I was afraid to ask for it.

I had no clue the man with whom I was speaking with was the president and chief executive officer (CEO) of the National Association of the Collard Pew (N.A.C.P. II), Kweisii Mfumey.

———

That day May in Washington, D.C., Alyson thought life had only just begun, although she had a full life before she met him; but in actuality life had only stopped like a possum in the road.

But would the Mandingo looking as if he was a direct descendant from the Mandinka tribe, walking in the gym restore Alyson to her former years? Only fate could paint such a perfect blend.

Alyson sniffed reality. But enjoy the moment was her motto. Don't live in the past while traveling in the present it blocks the joys of the future.

He sat behind Alyson and seemed to be more interested in the volleyball game than her.

He's playing hard to get. His cellular phone rings and Alyson ear is pained by the strong female voice vibrating through the speakers of the cell phone.

She peeped at him for some resolution — an answer. *Is that your girlfriend? Is she important? Can I take you from her or is she more confident, beautiful, and willing to love than I am?* His eyes offered no answers they only sealed the many knee jerking questions bombarding Alyson's pulse.

Quickly Janae's boyfriend clambered next to his dad, tall, dark brown and handsome, a replica of his dad. It was his mother inquiring as to his wear about.

More questions rambled through Alyson's mind. *Was that his wife? Is he married? I don't do married men. Where's the wedding ring? Or is he like the professional athletes they don't wear rings.* Alyson had her share of dating professional athletes. His persona said, "I'm single."

But Alyson had learned through the template of her soul not to accept personas. They were the sickening of the spirits, which dwelled within.

Several volleyball games past and each game Alyson's Mandingo appeared and each game he said little to no words to her. But he stared and smiled. His non-verbal message was briefly satisfying.

Each night Alyson traveled the long way home and meditated on her mysterious Mandingo while Tazzy blasted over the radio Chris Brown and Bow Wow *Shorty like Mine. The only thing that keeps me up when I'm feeling down. I don't know about you, but I gotta keep mines around.* Beyonce's *Irreplaceable. To the left, to the left everything you own in the box to the left. Standing in the front yard telling me how I'm such a fool. I'll never find a man like you...you must not know about me. I can have another you in a minute. As a matter of fact he'll be here in a minute.*

Alyson envied the days of youthfulness. She actually did have another one there in a minute. It was her ex-husband. Had he cursed her. When she left him for Kweisii he said, "You never find another man like me." Oh the power of words.

Time kept on "slipping into the future" and then low and behold the volleyball season had slipped away and so did Alyson's Mandingo. "No connection."

The basketball season was lurking around the corner, which meant Step Team practice for Tazzy, and the girls, and basketball practice for the boys. Maybe her Mandingo would reappear. He did. But so did the smell of reality.

Alyson determined not to make the same mistake with Kweisii, isolating herself, seeking answers from only information she gathered, began questioning people about her Mandingo, who she soon found out was a "Mandinga." *It was happening all over again. Why?*

The first wimps of the "no connection" was when Alyson telephoned him to speak to him before letting Tazzy attend a birthday party he was giving for his son. She gave Terrace Lurkins, "Boomer" her number and his dad insisted that Alyson called him. He didn't want to send the wrong message. He believed if he called Alyson she would think he liked her. "God forbid." He underestimated her intellectual abilities.

Alyson had a rule in her home that Tazzy could not attend a party or go to anyone's house without her making contact with the parents first. Some adults are sick enough to let children engage in sexual activities and drink alcohol.

Teens are too impressionable and incapable of logical thinking, because the frontal lobe revert it's development, this part of the brain controls logic.

Along with the pressure to grow up too fast, no teen should be trusted no matter how good they appear.

The second "no connection" blasted a few weeks later, when Alyson found a number written in a strange handwriting and called the number and then recognized his voice and immediately remembered it was the number given to her by his son.

She left a message stating she had found a number with no name and she was calling to inquire as to whose number it was. She did not want to hang up without saying anything. Because she did not want him to think she was playing on the telephone. The age of caller identification.

The third "no connection" siren at a Boe High School basketball game Tazzy and the crew were stepping. He attended and although he pointed Alyson out to several friends and flirted extensively, at the end of the game when he saw her standing alone he walked in the other direction. Kweisii all over again. *Can I escape this man? Loose the curse.*

The fourth "no connection" coiled in a splendid design. What happened to three strikes you are out? Boomer needed tutoring in science; a class, which may very well, had caused his freshman year basketball career.

Tazzy was recommended. Boomer asked Alyson and Alyson agreed to the tutoring with supervision. A schedule was arranged to begin tutoring. Although Boomer said it was okay, Alyson being the responsible person she was wanted to talk with the parents.

Remembering not to trust teenagers, and feeling closer to the dad than mom, Alyson approached the dad to confirm that it was okay to tutor his son.

She gave him her home telephone number and arrangements were made to do Saturday tutoring. Saturday came and went and Boomer was never delivered and there was no telephone call canceling the appointment or explaining the no show. A telephone call informing Alyson they could not make it would have been political correct. Not only was he on the down low but he was also rude. What an imperfect combination. Denial dies slowly but reality hits hard. The scales were removed from Alyson's eyes. She listened to the people's talk. Kweisii was not the only brother on the down low. They come a dime a dozen.

Only a few tears were shed over this one. Love was lost again. Many years later Alyson would wonder how she thought she could forsake a medical doctor for a fireman.

The holidays slipped quickly past the hourglass. Alyson silhouette figure reflected off the glistering glare off the apple-scented candle in her living room like a mural. The mauve wing chair gave her no support. She was restless. The telephone rung.

"Hello. May I speak to Alyson?"

"Speaking."

"How have you been doing?"

"Okay." She did not want to lie. She was beginning to lose weight again. She had cut her hair extremely short. All over.

"Just okay. I have not heard from you in awhile so I thought I would call you and make sure everything," he paused, "is okay."

Who is this? Chip? Chip had called to apologize for his role in Kweisii's messy mess. He had no remorse about Kweisii's fate.

He was just glad Alyson had never mentioned his nor Tommy, Kweisii's baby boy, for the role in the kidnapping and rape. Alyson knew they were being blind-sided.

"Who is this?"

"Oh. I'm sorry it's Germaine."

"Oh." She had forgot his voice. How could she?

Nervously he continued. "Well, if everything is okay I won't keep you."

Alyson inhaled reality. "No! No don't hang up. I'm sorry. I was just sitting here in my living room dozing off. I'm awake now. Wide awake."

"Well, I'm in the area and was wondering if you would mind if I came over and visited you." A long silent pause. "I would really like to see you. It's been a long time."

A long time coming but a change is going to come.

"I don't mind."

"I'll be there in approximately twenty-five minutes."

Alyson laughed finally. She imagined him in the small town twenty-five miles off the shore of her home, at a red light where cell phone reception was clear waiting for the go or no go signal. This time it was a go. The light turned green.

Exactly thirty minutes later the doorbell rung. Alyson who normally answered the door make-up less, sweat pants and big sweatshirt, had showered, quickly, applied make-up that made her hazel eyes sparkled in the sunlight giving off a teal blue falsetto. She trimmed her lips in plum lip liner and lined her lips in gold, and her check blush rose. The glow was permanent.

She wore Tommy Hilfiger stretch jeans and Liz Claiborne black sweater and Ecco leather clogs. She did not carry a bag to the door. She needed to be set free.

The door flew open and into the arms of Dr. Germaine "Germany" Ruiz she collapsed. She should be so happy.

Round ten her demons were knocked out.

www.ingramcontent.com/pod-product-compliance
Lightning Source LLC
Chambersburg PA
CBHW031201020726
47499CB00002B/442